HIPPOCRENE HANDY DICTIONARIES

Arabic

HIPPOCRENE HANDY DICTIONARIES

For the traveler of independent spirit and curious mind, this practical series will help you to communicate, not just get by. Easier to use than a dictionary, the comprehensive listing of words and phrases is arranged alphabetically by key word. More versatile than a phrasebook, words frequently met in stores, on signs, or needed for standard replies, are conveniently presented by subject.

ARABIC
ISBN 0-87052-960-9

PORTUGUESE
ISBN 0-87052-053-9

CHINESE
ISBN 0-87052-050-4

THAI
ISBN 0-87052-963-3

DUTCH
ISBN 0-87052-049-0

TURKISH
ISBN 0-87052-982-X

GREEK
ISBN 0-87052-961-7

SERBO-CROATIAN
ISBN 0-87052-051-2

JAPANESE
ISBN 0-87052-962-5

SWEDISH
ISBN 0-87052-054-7

Books may be ordered directly from the publisher. Each book costs $6.95. Send the total amount plus $3.50 for shipping and handling to:　　Hippocrene Books, Inc.
　　　　　171 Madison Avenue
　　　　　New York, NY 10016.

HIPPOCRENE HANDY DICTIONARIES

Arabic

compiled by

LEXUS

with

Adel Ezzeldin and Janet Leng

HIPPOCRENE BOOKS
New York

Published in the United States of America in 1991 by
HIPPOCRENE BOOKS, INC., New York,
by arrangement with Routledge, London

For information, address:
HIPPOCRENE BOOKS, INC.
171 Madison Ave.
New York, NY 10016

ISBN 0-87052-960-9

Contents

Introduction

Classical Arabic, the language of the Koran, is the universal *written* language of the entire Arab world. It is quite complex and many native Arabic speakers find it very difficult. It is rarely spoken and should certainly not be encountered by the visitor in his everyday dealings within an Arab country.

Colloquial Arabic is the language *spoken* by Arab peoples. It varies tremendously between countries in grammar, vocabulary and pronunciation although its written form remains constant. The Egyptian variety of colloquial Arabic used in this book is well recognized through the spread of popular films and songs. It is, fortunately, much simpler than Classical Arabic. Indeed a speaker of Egyptian colloquial Arabic will always try to avoid complicated constructions and will attempt to say things in the simplest possible way. English-speakers should find word order and sentence structure fairly familiar.

Egyptians, living as they do at the crossroads of the Middle East, are more than accustomed to hearing a wide variation of speech. You are likely to find every effort made to understand your attempts at the language. This tolerance and the preferred simplicity of Egyptian Arabic should encourage visitors to make a confident approach to the Arabic language from the very beginning of their stay.

THE ARABIC ALPHABET

This table shows the letters of the Arabic alphabet in the different forms they take according to their position in a word. The righthand column is the equivalent English sound as used in the pronunciation system in this book.

Final	Median	Initial	Isolated	
ا	ا	أ ـ ا	أ	a
ب	ـبـ	بـ	ب	b
ت	ـتـ	تـ	ت	t
ث	ـثـ	ثـ	ث	s
ج	ـجـ	جـ	ج	g
ح	ـحـ	حـ	ح	H
خ	ـخـ	خـ	خ	kh
د	ـد	د	د	d
ذ	ـذ	ذ	ذ	z
ر	ـر	ر	ر	r
ز	ـز	ز	ز	z
س	ـسـ	سـ	س	s
ش	ـشـ	شـ	ش	sh
ص	ـصـ	صـ	ص	s
ض	ـضـ	ضـ	ض	d
ط	ـطـ	ط	ط	t
ظ	ـظـ	ظ	ظ	z
ع	ـعـ	عـ	ع	*
غ	ـغـ	غـ	غ	gh
ف	ـفـ	فـ	ف	f
ق	ـقـ	قـ	ق	k
ك	ـكـ	كـ	ك	k
ل	ـلـ	لـ	ل	l
م	ـمـ	مـ	م	m
ن	ـنـ	نـ	ن	n
و	و	و	و	w
ة ـه	ـهـ	هـ	ة	h
ى	ـيـ	يـ	ى	y
ڤ	ـڤـ	ڤـ	ڤ	v
چ	ـچـ	چـ	چ	SH

Final   Median   Initial   Isolated

Pronunciation Guide

Although written Arabic is the same throughout the Arabic world, there are differences in pronunciation. The Arabic translations in this book have been written in a pronunciation system which reflects the spoken language that you will encounter in Egypt. You will, however, find that this way of speaking Arabic is generally familiar to people throughout the Arabic world largely as a result of films and television. Where a translation is given in quotes this means that the pronunciation is more or less equivalent to the English pronunciation of the word. Where one or two letters are given in bold type this means that this part of the word should be stressed.

VOWELS

a	as in 'cat'		I	as in 'eye' or 'night'
ā	similar to the 'a' in 'cat' but longer		o	as in 'not'
aa	as in 'car'		ō	as in 'moment'
ay	as in 'may'		oo	as in 'boot'
e	as in 'met'		ow	as in 'now'
ē	as in 'pair'		u	as in 'bull'
ee	as in 'meet'		uh	as in 'mud'
i	as in 'sit'			

Arabic vowels should always be pronounced with equal clarity and never swallowed as often happens in English with, for example, the last syllable of 'seven'.

CONSONANTS

h	is always pronounced – except when occurring in the following combinations: gh, kh, sh, sH, th, uh
kh	as in the Scottish pronunciation of 'loch'
p	only occurs in loan words and will be pronounced 'b' by Egyptians
r	must be strongly rolled and never silent as in English
s	as in 'so' or 'hiss', never as in 'advise'
sH	as the 's' sound in 'pleasure'

A double consonant such as 'tt' or 'nn' should be sounded twice – as in Italian.

SPECIAL SOUNDS

gh	as a French 'r'
H	an emphatic 'h'; you should forcibly breathe out from your throat while pronouncing this sound
'	glottal stop; as often heard in regional forms of English when the letter 't' is omitted, as for example in 'ho' wa'er bo'le' for 'hot water bottle'
*	this sound is much more difficult to describe than it is to produce; it represents the letter 'ine' in Arabic; imagine making the classic comic strip scream 'aaaaaagh' straight from your throat; if you can now produce the same sound but very briefly you should be making the right sound; it will become much easier if you do not worry about the sound in isolation; instead try to use it quickly and blend it into any following vowel, usually an 'a', to modify the overall sound

English-Arabic

A

a: 20 piastres a bottle *ashreen uhrsh el ezaza; *see page 102*

about: about 25 Hawālee khamsa wa *ashreen; **about 6 o'clock** Hawālee e-sa*a sitta; **is the manager about?** el modeer mowgood?; **I was just about to leave** ana kunt lessa mashee; **how about a drink?** teshrab ay?

above fō'; **above 5** fō' khamsa

abroad (*go*) lil khareg; (*live*) fil khareg

abscess dimil

absolutely: it's absolutely perfect da tamam awee; **you're absolutely right** inta *ala Ha'; **absolutely!** kuht*an!

absorbent cotton otna tebbee

accelerator dawāsit benzeen

accept mowafi'

accident Hadsa; **there's been an accident** kan fee Hadsa; **sorry, it was an accident** asif ghuhsb *anee

accommodation(s) sakken; **we need accommodation(s) for four** *a-izeen sakken lay arba*a

accurate mazboot

ace (*cards*) uhs

ache: I have an ache here *andee waga* hena; **it aches** bitooga*

across *abr; **across the street** *abr e-shari*a

actor momasil

actress momasilla

adapter (*electrical*) *not generally available — advisable to take your own*

address *inwān; **what's your address?** *inwānak ay?

address book kitab *anaween

admission: how much is admission? e-dikhool bikam?

adore: I adore ... (*this country, this food etc*) ana baHebb ...

adult sheb

advance: I'll pay in advance Hadfa* mō'adam

advertisement e*alēn

advise: what would you advise? inta ra'yak ay?

aeroplane tiyara

affluent baHbooH

afraid: I'm afraid of heights ana bakhef min el *iloo; **don't be afraid** matkhefsh; **I'm not afraid** ana mush khayf; **I'm afraid I can't help you** asif mush Ha'dar asa*duhk; **I'm afraid so** lil asif; **I'm afraid not** la'

after ba*d; **after 9 o'clock** ba*d e-sa*a tis*a; **after you** ba*dak

afternoon ba*d e-dohr; **in the afternoon** fil dohraya; **good afternoon** misē' el kheer; **this afternoon** e-dohraya

aftershave lōshan

afterwards ba*dayn

again mara tania

against duhd

age *omr; **under age** moraahek; **not at my age!** mush fee sinee!; **it takes ages** bitakhud wa't taweel; **I haven't been here for ages** ana magetsh hena min zamān

agency wikāla

aggressive *adwānee

ago: a year ago min sana; **it wasn't long ago** mush min moda taweela

agony: it's agony alam shedeed

agree: do you agree? inta mowafi'?; **I agree** ana mowafi'; **it doesn't agree with me** matwafi'neesh

1

AIDS 'AIDS'
air howa; **by air** bi tIyara
air-conditioning takeef howa
air hostess modeefa gawaya
airmail: by airmail bil bareed e-gawee
airmail envelope zurf bareed gawee
airplane tIyara
airport mataar
airport bus ōtōbees el mataar
airport tax dareebit el mataar
alabaster rokham
alarm inzaar
alarm clock minnabeh
alcohol koHol
alcoholic: is it alcoholic? da koHollee?
Alexandria iskindraya
Algeria el gazē'ir
Algerian (man, adjective) gaze'eeree; (woman) gaze'eeraya
Algiers el gazē'ir
alive *a-Iyish; **is he still alive?** hoowa lessa *a-Iyish?
all kul; **all the hotels** kul el fanādi'; **all my friends** kul asHaabee; **all my money** kul floosee; **all of it** kuloo; **all of them** kuloohum; **all right** kuloo tamam; **I'm all right** ana kwIyis; **that's all** bas kedda; **it's all changed** kuloo etghIyar; **thank you — not at all** shukran — el *afw
Allah allah; **praise be to Allah** el Hamdu lillah
allergic: I'm allergic to ... ana Hassas lil ...
allergy Hassasaya
alligator timseH
all-inclusive kuloo maHsoob fee
allowed masmōH; **is it allowed?** da masmōH?; **I'm not allowed to eat salt** ana mamnoo-a* min akl el malH
all-risks (insurance) kul el akhtaar
almost ta'reeban
alone waHeed; **are you alone?** inta li waHdak?; **leave me alone** sibnee li waHdee
already min abl
also kamen

alteration ta*deel
alternative: is there an alternative? fee badeel?; **we had no alternative** makensh *andenna badeel
alternator mō-walid kaharaabee
although bilraaghm min
altogether kuloohum; **what does that come to altogether?** kuloohum bikam?
always dIman
a.m.: at 8 a.m. e-sa*a tamania e-subH
amazing modhish
ambassador safeer
ambulance is*af; **get an ambulance** otlub el is*af
America amreeka
American (adjective) amreekee; (man) amreekānee; (woman) amreekanaya; **the Americans** el amreekan
American plan ikaama kamla
amoebic dysentery dusunteree-a, 'amoeba'
among bayn
an(a)esthetic beng
ancestors gedood
anchor helb
anchovies anshooga
ancient adeem
and wa
angina dee' nafas
angry za*lēn; **I'm very angry about it** ana za*lēn awee
animal HIawan
ankh ank
ankle asabit e-rigl (f)
anniversary *Iyeed; **it's our (wedding) anniversary today** *Iyeed zawagna e-sanawee e-naharda
annoy: he's annoying me hoowa midaye'nee; **it's so annoying** dee Haga tidayi'
another: can we have another room? mumkin ōda tania?; **another bottle, please** ezaza tania lowsamaHt
answer: there was no answer makensh fee ruhd; **what was his answer?** radoo kan ay?
ant: ants naml
antibiotics bensileen

antihistamine 'allergex' (*tm*)
antique: is it an antique? da anteek?
antique shop maHal anteeka
antiquities asaar
antisocial: don't be antisocial mateb'ash baykh
any: have you got any bread/milk? *andak *I-esh/laban?; **I haven't got any** ma*andeesh
anybody: can anybody help me? mumkin Had yisa*Idnee?; **there wasn't anybody there** makensh fee Had hinak
anything aya Haga; **I don't want anything** mush *a-Iyiz Haga; **don't you have anything else?** *andak Haga tania?
apart from monfassil
apartment sha'a
aperitif mashroobaat li fatH e-shahaya
apology e*atizaar; **please accept my apologies** e'bel e*atizaree lowsamaHt
appalling mor*ayb
appear: it would appear that ... min el waadeH en ...
appendicitis el a*war
appetite shahaya; **I've lost my appetite** maleesh nifs
apple tufaHa
application form taluhb ta'deem
appointment ma*ad; **I'd like to make an appointment** *a-Iyiz aHgiz ma*ad
appreciate: thank you, I appreciate it shukran giddan giddan
approve: she doesn't approve haya mush moo-waf'a
apricot mishmisha
April abreel
aqualung gehaz tanafuhs
Arab (*man, adjective*) *arabee; (*woman*) *arabaya; **the Arabs** el *arab
Arabic (*adjective*) *arabee; (*language*) lōgha *arabaya
Arab League el gam*a el *arabaya
arch(a)eology asaar
are *see page 113*
area: I don't know the area ana mush *arif el monti'a

area code nimrit el monti'a
arm dira*
around *see* **about**
arrangement: will you make the arrangements? mumkin te*amil el lēzim?
arrest abuhd *ala; **he's been arrested** hoowa it'abuhd *alay
arrival wisool
arrive: when do we arrive? Hanewsuhl emta?; **has my parcel arrived yet?** e-tard bita*ee wasuhl?; **let me know as soon as they arrive** ollee awil mIyoosuhl; **we only arrived yesterday** eHna wasuhlna imbarraH bas
art fan
art gallery saalit *ard el finoon
arthritis eltihab el mafassil
artichoke kharshoofa
artificial (*man-made*) istin*I; (*false*) moozayif
artist fanān
as: as fast as you can biasra* mIyumkin; **as much as you can** *ala ad mati'dar; **as you like** *ala kayfak; **as it's getting late** le'en el wa't mit'akhuhr
ashore lil shuht
ashtray tuhfIya
aside from monfassil
ask taluhb; **that's not what I asked for** ana mataluhbtish da; **could you ask him to phone back?** mumkin ti'olloo yitessil baya?
asleep: he's still asleep hoowa lessa nayim
aspirin asbreen
assault: she's been assaulted it-hagam *alayha; **indecent assault** hegoom faadeH
assistant (*helper*) moosayId; (*in shop*) (*male*) baya*; (*female*) baya*a
assume: I assume that ... ana azon en ...
asthma azma
astonishing modhish
Aswan aswaan
at: at the café *and el ahwa; **at the**

hotel *and el fondō'; **at 8 o'clock e-sa*a** tamania; **see you at dinner** ashoofak fil *asha
Atlantic Ocean el moнeed el atlantee
Atlas Mountains gibal uhtluhs
atmosphere (*weather*) e-gow
attractive нelw; **you're very attractive** (*to a woman*) intee нelwa awee
aubergine bitingaana
auction mazad *alanee
audience guhmhoor
August aghostos
aunt (*mother's sister*) khēlla; (*father's sister*) *amma
Australia ostralya
Australian (*man, adjective*) osturaalee; (*woman*) osturalaya
Austria e-nimsa
authorities e-sultaat
automatic ōtoomateekee

automobile *arabaya
autumn khareef; **in the autumn** fil khareef
available: when will it be available? emta нıkoon gēhiz?; **when will he be available?** emta нıkoon faadee?
avenue taree' mashuhguhr
average: the average Egyptian el masree el *adee; **an above average hotel** fondō' fō' el mōtawassit; **a below average hotel** fondō' taнt el mōtawassit; **the food was only average** el akl kan ma*ool; **on average** bimoo*adil
awake: is she awake? haya saнaya?
away: is it far away? da ba*yeed?; **go away!** imshee!
awful fazee-a*
axle (*front*) meнwar amāmee; (*rear*) meнwar khalfee

B

baby noonoo, 'baby'
baby-carrier 'carrycot'
baby-sitter dada; **can you get us a baby-sitter?** mumkin tegeeb lenna dada?
bachelor *azib
back (*of body*) dahr; **I've got a bad back** dahree mush kwıyis; **at the back** fil akher; **I'll be right back** нarga* *alatool; **when do you want it back?** *a-ızhoo emta?; **can I have my money back?** mumkin ekhud floosee?; **come back!** erga*!; **I go back home tomorrow** ana merowaн bukra; **we'll be back next year** нanerga*a e-sana e-gaya; **when is the last bus back?** emta akher ōtōbees?
backache: I have a backache *andee waga* fi dahree

back door bab waraanee
backgammon towla
backpack shanta li dahr
back seat korsee akher
bad: you are bad inta mo'zee; **this meat's bad** el laнma dee fazda; **a bad headache** suda* shedeed; **it's not bad** ma*ool; **too bad!** waнesh awee
badly: he's been badly injured e-sabtoo radee'a
bag (*suitcase*) shanta; (*carrier bag*) kees
baggage shōnuht
baggage allowance wazna magēnee
baggage checkroom maktab el amanēt
Bahrain el baнrayn
bakery foruhn
balcony (*in cinema*) balakōn; (*of house*) balakōna; **a room with a balcony**

oda bee balakōna; **on the balcony** fil balakōna
bald a'ra*
ball kora
ballet 'ballet'
ball-point pen alam gaf
banana mooza
band (*music*) fer'a
bandage roobaat shesh; **could you change the bandage?** mumkin tighayar roobaat e-shesh?
bandaid shireet laza'
bank bank; **when is the bank open?** el bank beeyeftaH emta?
bank account Hisaab fil bank
bar 'bar'; **let's meet in the bar** mumkin nit'aabil fil 'bar'; **a bar of chocolate** shokalaata
barbecued meats laHma meshwaya
barber salōn Hila'a
bargain: it's a real bargain dee lo'ta Ha'ee-ee
barman garsōn
barrette bensa; (*with fancy decoration*) tooka
bartender garsōn
basic assassee; **the hotel is rather basic** el fondō' *adee khalis; **will you teach me some basic phrases?** mumkin te*alimnee ba*d e-gomal el assasaya?
basket (*storage*) afuhs; (*for shopping*) saabat
bath banyō; **can I take a bath?** mumkin asta*mil el banyō; **could you give me a bath towel?** mumkin teddeenee footit el Hammem?
bathing costume mayoo
bathrobe rōb Hammem
bathroom Hammem; **a room with a private bathroom** ōda bi Hammem; **can I use your bathroom?** mumkin e-tawalet, lowsamaHt?
battery battaraya; **the battery's flat** el battaraya fadia
bay khaleeg
bazaar soo'
be: be reasonable kheleek ma*ool; **don't be lazy** mateb'ash kaslān;

where have you been? (*to a man*) kunt fayn?; (*to a woman*) kuntee fayn?; **I've never been to Luxor** ana *omree maroHt lu'suhr; *see page 113*
beach bilasH; **on the beach** *alel bilasH; **I'm going to the beach** ana rIaH lil bilasH
beach mat Haseerit bilasH
beach towel footit bilasH
beach umbrella shamsayit bilasH
beads kharaz
beans (*green*) fasōlya; (*dried*) lobya; (*brown, dried*) fool
beard da'n (*f*)
beautiful gameel; **thank you, that's beautiful** shukran da Helwa awee
beauty salon salōn tagmeel
because *alashen; **because of the weather** bisabab e-gow
bed sireer; **single bed** sireer; **twin beds** sireerayn; **double bed** sireer litneen; **you haven't made my bed** ma*amalteesh sireeree; **he's still in bed** hoowa lessa fi sireer; **I'm going to bed** ana dekhil anam
bed and breakfast noom wiftar
bed linen bIyadaat
bedroom ōt e-noom
Beduin badawee; **the Beduin** badoo
bee naHla
beef fillay
beer beera; **two beers, please** ezaztayn beera, lowsamaHt
before abl; **before breakfast** abl el fetar; **before I leave** abl mamshee; **I haven't been here before** ana *omree magayt hena
beggar shaHat
begin: when does it begin? bitebda' emta?
beginner mobtadi'; **I'm just a beginner** ana lessa mobtadi'
beginning: at the beginning fil beedaya
behavio(u)r tasaruf
behind wara; **the driver behind me** e-saweh' ellee warIya
beige baysH
Beirut 'Beirut'

believe: I don't believe you ana mush misada'ak; **I believe you** ana misada'ak

bell guhras

belly-dance ra's shar'ee

bellydancer ra'aasa

belly-dancing ra's shar'ee

belong: that belongs to me da bita*ee; **who does this belong to?** da bita*a meen?

belongings: all my belongings kuloo mumtalakaatee

below taHt; **below the knee** taHt e-rukba; **below 50** a'al min khamseen

belt (clothing) Hezam

bend (in road) malaf

berth (on ship) sireer

beside gamb; **beside the mosque** gamb e-gâmi*a; **sit beside me** o*ad gambee

besides: besides that kamen

best aHsen; **the best hotel in town** aHsen fondô' fil muhnti'a; **that's the best meal I've ever had** dee aHsen akla kalteha

bet rahan; **I bet you 50 piastres** arahnak khamseen uhrsh

better aHsen; **that's better!** kedda aHsen; **are you feeling better?** inta Kwiyis?; **I'm feeling a lot better now** ana aHsen delwa'tee; **I'd better be going now** ana lezim amshee delwa'tee

between bayn

beyond ab*ad min; **beyond the desert** ab*ad min e-saHara

bicycle *agala; **can we rent bicycles here?** mumkin ni'guhr *agal hena?

big kebeer; **a big one** kebeer; **that's too big** da kebeer awee; **it's not big enough** (too short) osiyar awee; (too small) sooghiyar awee; (not enough) mush kifaya

bigger akbar; **do you have a bigger one?** *andak aya Haga akbar?

bike *agala

bikini bikeenee

bilharzia bilharissya

bill fatoora; **could I have the bill,**

please? mumkin el fatoora, lowsamaHt?

billfold maHfaza

billiards bileeyardô

birds teeyor

biro (tm) alam gaf

birthday *iyeed milad; **it's my birthday** *iyeed miladee; **when is your birthday?** *iyeed miladuhk emta?; **happy birthday!** *iyeed milad sa*yeed!

biscuit baskaweet

bit Hetta; **just a little bit for me** Hetta sooghiyara; **a big bit** Hetta kebeera; **a bit of that cake** Hetta min el kayk da; **it's a bit too big for me** (in size) da kebeer awee; (in quantity) da keteer awee; **it's a bit cold today** e-naharda bard shwiya

bite (by insect) uhrsa; (by animal) *ada; **I've been bitten** (by insect) ana et'aruhst; (by dog) kalb *adinee; **do you have something for insect bites?** *andak Haga li ars el Hasharaat?

bitter (taste) morr

bitter lemon lamoon morr

black eswid; **black and white film** film abee-ad wi eswid

blackout: he's had a blackout hoowa oghma *alay

bladder mathuhna; (colloquial word) massuhna

blanket batanaya; **I'd like another blanket, please** batanaya tania lowsamaHt

blazer bilayzar

bleach (for toilet etc) bitahs

bleed: he's bleeding damoo sayyeH

bless you! (after sneeze) *anoo!

blind a*ama

blinds sattayar

blister kees miya

blocked (road, drain) mazdood

block of flats *omara

blond (hair) asfuhr; (colouring) ash'ar

blonde (noun) sha'ra

blood dam; **his blood group is ...** damoo magmoo*a ...; **I have high**

blood pressure *andee erteefa*a fi daght e-dam

blouse bilooza

blue azra'

blusher (*cosmetic*) bankeek

board: full board ikaama kamla; **half-board** nus ikaama

boarding house benseeyōn

boarding pass bita'it so*ood

boat markib; **Egyptian sailing boat** felooka

body gisma

boil (*on body*) dimil; **boil the water** eghlee el mīya

boiled egg bayda masloo'a

boiling hot (*weather, food*) sukhn narr

bomb (*noun*) kombilla

bone (*in meat, body*) *adma; (*in fish*) shōka

bonnet (*of car*) kaboot

book (*noun*) kitab; **I'd like to book a table for two** mumkin aнgiz tarabayza litneen

bookshop, bookstore maktaba

boot (*on foot*) boot; (*of car*) shanta

booze koнol; **I had too much booze** ana shribt keteer

border (*of country*) нedood

bored: I'm bored ana zeh'en

boring mumil

born: I was born in ... (*date/place*) ana etwalat fi ...

borrow: may I borrow ...? mumkin estayeer; (*money*) mumkin estelif ...?

boss rīyis

both: I'll take both of them нakhud litneen; **we'll both come** eнna litneen нaneegee

bother: sorry to bother you asif *alel iz*ag; **it's no bother** mush mōhim; **it's such a bother** da kuloo mata*ıb

bottle ezaza; **a bottle of wine** ezazit nebeez; **another bottle, please** ezaza tania lowsamaнt

bottle-opener fatēнa

bottom (*base*) a*ada; **at the bottom of the Pyramids** *and a*dit el нaram

bottom gear elowel

bouncer (*at club*) fitowaa (*m*)

bowels masareen

box sandoo'

box office shebek tazēkir

boy walad

boyfriend: my boyfriend saнibee

bra sinteeyen

bracelet iswera

brake fluid zayt faraamil

brake lining bitaanit el faraamil

brakes faraamil; **there's something wrong with the brakes** fee *ıyib fil faraamil; **can you check the brakes?** mumkin tekshif *alel faraamil?; **I had to brake suddenly** edtarayt afaarmil bisora*a

brandy 'cognac'

brass naнas asfar; **made of brass** min e-naнas

brave shuga*

bread *ı-esh; **could we have some bread and butter?** mumkin *ı-esh wee zebda?; **some more bread, please** *ı-esh tanee, lowsamaнt; **white bread** feenō; **wholemeal bread** *ı-esh baladee; **white pitta bread** *ı-esh shāmee

break kuhsuhr; **I think I've broken my ankle** azon inee kuhsuhrt asabit riglee; **it keeps breaking** dıman titkuhsuhr

breakdown: I've had a breakdown (*in a car*) *arabeetee et*atalit; **nervous breakdown** inheeyar *asabee

breakfast fetar; **English breakfast** fetar ingileezee; **full breakfast** fetar kaamil; **continental breakfast** fetar 'continental'

break in: somebody's broken in нaraamee dakhel hena

breast (*chest*) sedr; (*woman's breast*) bez

breast-feed reeda*a

breath nafas; **out of breath** mafeesh nafas

breathe: I can't breathe mush adir atnafis

breathtaking museer

breeze nisma

bridal suite ginaн el *arsen

bride *aroosa
bridegroom *arees
bridge (over river) kubree
brief (stay, visit) mokhtassir
briefly bekhtisaar
briefcase shanta
bright (colour) zaahee; bright red
aʜmar zaahee
brilliant (idea) momtaz; (colour) moo-
wahwig
bring gab; could you bring it to my
hotel? mumkin tegeeboo lil fondō'
bita*ee?; I'll bring it back ana
ʜaraga*oo; can I bring a friend
too? mumkin ageeb saʜbee ma*aya?
Britain ingilterra
British ingileezee; the British el
ingileez
brochure matboo-*a; do you have
any brochures on ...? *andak
matboo-*aat *an ...?
broke: I'm broke ana mifalis
broken maksoor; you've broken it
inta kasartoo; it's broken maksoor;
broken nose anf maksoor
brooch brōsʜ
brother akh; my brother akhooya
brother-in-law: my brother-in-law
(wife's brother) akhoo miraatee; (husband's brother) akhoo goozee
brown bonee; I don't go brown ana
mabasmarsh
browse: may I just browse around?
mumkin atfarag?
bruise (noun) waram azra'
brunette bonee
brush (noun) forsha
bucket gardel
buffalo gamoosa
buffet 'buffet'
bug (insect) ʜashara; bed bugs ba';
she's caught a bug *andaha a*adwa
building mabna
bulb (electrical) luhnda; a new bulb
luhnda gedeeda
bull *a-ɪgl
bullfrog dovda*a
bulrushes nabat el baardee
bump khabt; I bumped my head

khabat raasee
bumper ekseedaam
bumpy (road, flight) matabaat
bunch of flowers bookay ward
bungalow bayt ardee
bunion tawalwul fi rigl
bunk beds sireer bidoorayn
buoy *awaama
burglar ʜaraamee
burn ʜar'; do you have an ointment
for burns? *andak maraham lil
ʜuroo'?
burnt maʜroo'; this meat is burnt el
laʜma dee maʜuroo'a; my arms are
so burnt diroo*ɪ maʜuroo'a awee
burst: a burst pipe masoora mifar'a*a
bus ōtōbees; is this the bus for ...? el
ōtōbees da rɪyaʜ ...?; when's the
next bus? (while at stop) el ōtōbees
gay emta?; (when booking) emta el
ōtōbees ellee ba*dō?
bus driver sawē' ōtōbees
business shoghl; I'm here on business ana hena fi shoghl; it's a
pleasure to do business with you
yisharuhfnee el *amil ma*a seeyatak
bus station mow'af ōtōbees
bus stop maʜatit ōtōbees; will you
tell me which bus stop I get off at?
mumkin ti'ollee anzil fayn?
bust (of body) sedr
bus tour gowla mōnazuhma
busy (street, restaurant) masʜghool;
I'm busy this evening ana
masʜghool elleelādee; the line was
busy (telephone) el khad kan
masʜghool
but laakin; not ... but ... mush ...
laakin ...
butcher guhzar
butter zebda
butterfly faraasha
button zoorar
buy: I'll buy it ʜashteree; where can
I buy ...? fayn ashteree ...?
by bil; by boat bil markib; by car bil
*arabaya; by train bil atr; who's it
written by? meen kataboo?; I came
by myself gayt lee waʜdee; a seat

by the window korsee gamb e-shebek; **by the sea** gamb el baнr; **can you do it by Wednesday?**

mumkin te*amiloo *ala yum el arba*?
bye-bye 'bye-bye'

C

cab (*taxi*) taksee; (*fixed price from airport*) limōzeen
cabaret 'cabaret'
cabbage kuromba
cabin kabeena
cable (*electrical*) silk kaharaba
café ahwa
caffeine 'caffeine'
Cairo el kaheera
cake kayk; **a piece of cake** нettit kayk
calculator 'calculator'
calendar nateega
caliph khaleefa (*m*); **tombs of the caliphs** ma'aabir el khaleefa
call: what is this called? da ismoo ay?; **call the manager!** inda el modeer!; **I'd like to make a call to England** ana *a-ıyiz a*mil mokalma lingilterra; **I'll call back later** (*come back*) нarga* tanee; (*phone back*) нatessil tanee; **I'm expecting a call from London** ana mestannee mokalma min 'london'; **would you give me a call at 7.30?** mumkin tetessil baya e-sa*a saba*a wi nus?; **it's been called off** itlagha
call box telefōn
calm (*person, sea*) hedee; **calm down!** ehedda!
Calor gas (*tm*) uhnboobit bootagaz
calories waнedaat нarraraya
camel gamal
camel driver ra*ee e-gimāl
camel racing sibe' e-gimāl
camel ride: how much is a camel ride to the sphinx? bikam lee aboo el нōl?; **I'd like to ride a camel — how much is it?** ana *a-ıyiz arkab gamal — bikam?
camel train kaafillit gimāl
camera 'camera'
camp: is there somewhere we can camp? fee makken mumkin nay*askuhr fee?; **can we camp here?** mumkin nay*askuhr hena?
campbed sireer khayma
camping takheem
campsite ma*askuhr shebeb
can (*tin*) safeeнa; **a can of mango juice** *albit manga
can: can I ...? mumkin ana ...?; **can you ...?** mumkin inta ...?; **can he ...?** mumkin hoowa ...?; **can she ...?** mumkin haya ...?; **can we ...?** mumkin eнna ...?; **can they ...?** mumkin humma ...?; **I can't ...** ma'adarsh ...; **he can't ... hoowa** mayi'darsh ...; **can I keep it?** mumkin aнtuhfiz bee?; **if I can** lowa'dar; **that can't be right** da ghalat
Canada 'canada'
Canadian (*man, adjective*) kanadee; (*woman*) kanadaya
cancel lagha; **can I cancel my reservation?** mumkin elghee el нagz bita*ee?; **can we cancel dinner for tonight?** mumkin nilghee el *asha elleelādee?; **I cancelled it** ana laghaytoo
cancellation ghe'
candle sham*a
candies (*in wrappers*) bon bon; (*general term for sweets*) нalawee-at; **a piece of candy** нettit нalawee-at
can-opener fataнa

cap ghuhtaa; **bathing cap** bonnay lil sibaHa
capital city el medeena e-ra'eesaya
capital letters Haroof kebeera
capsize: it capsized it'alabit
captain (*of ship*) 'captain'
car *arabaya
carafe 'carafe'
carat: is it 9/14 carat gold? da *ayar tis*a/arba*ataashar?
caravan (*of camels*) kaafilla
carbonated fawarr
carburet(t)or kaarbrete-ir
card: do you have a (business) card? ma*ak kart?
cardboard box *alba kartōn
cardigan bullōvar maftooHa
cards kutsheena; **do you play cards?** bitil*ab kutsheena?
care: goodbye, take care ma*a salemma, khelee baalak min nafsak; **will you take care of this bag for me?** mumkin tekhud baalak min e-shanta dee?; **care of ...** bitaruhf ...
careful: be careful! khelee baalak!
careless: that was careless of you da ehmal minak; **careless driving** seewaa' bi ehmal
car ferry ma*adaya
car hire ta'geer *arabeeyaat
car keys mufatiyaH el *arabaya
carnation oronfil
carnival 'carnival'
car park mow'af *arabeeyaat
carpet sigada
car rental (*place*) maktab ta'geer *arabeeyaat
carriage (*with horse*) Hantoor
carrots guhzuhr
carry shel; **could you carry this for me?** mumkin tisheel da *alashēnee?
carry-all shanta
carry-cot 'carrycot'
car-sick: I get car-sick ana *andee dawakhen safar
Carthage kortaag
carton kartōn; **a carton of milk** kartōnet laban
carving naHt

carwash gheseel *arabaya
Casablanca e-daar el bIdaa'
case (*suitcase*) shanta; **in any case** fee ay Hala; **in that case** fil Hala dee; **it's a special case** dee Hala khasa; **in case he comes back** fee Haalet reegoo*a tanee; **I'll take two just in case** Hakhud itneen lil Huhrs
cash feloos; **I don't have any cash** ma*eesh feloos; **I'll pay cash** Hatfa*kesh; **will you cash a cheque/check for me?** mumkin tesriflee sheek?
cashdesk (*in shop*) kays
cash dispenser el bank e-shakhsee
cash register khazna
casino 'casino'
cassette 'cassette'
cassette player, cassette recorder tazgeel
castle asr
casual: casual clothes malābis shebab
cat ota
catacombs saradeeb
catamaran 'catamaran'
catastrophe museeba
catch: where do we catch the bus? minayn nakhud el ōtōbees?; **he's caught some strange illness** hoowa *andoo marad ghereeb mo*adee
catching: is it catching? da mo*adee?
cathedral kattedra-aya
Catholic (*adjective*) kathlik
cauliflower aranabeet
cause sabab
cave maghara
caviar koviar
ceiling sa'f
celebrations eHtifel
cellophane suloofen
cemetery madfen; (*historic, Islamic*) ma'aabir
center west; *see also* **centre**
centigrade ma'awaya; *see page 119*
centimetre, centimeter 'centimetre'; *see page 117*
central ra'eesee; **we'd prefer something more central** eHna nifaduhl Haga fee west el balad

central station el maHatta e-ra'eesaya
centre west; **how do we get to the centre?** izay noosal li west el balad?; **in the centre (of town)** fee west el balad
century meet sana; **in the 19th century** fil arn e-tisa*taashar; **in the 20th century** fil arn el *ashreen
ceramics khazaf
certain mutakid; **are you certain?** inta mutakid?; **I'm absolutely certain** ana mutakid awee
certainly tab*an; **certainly not** la' tab*an
certificate shaheda; **birth certificate** shahedit meelad
chain (for bike) ganzeer; (around neck) silsilla
chair korsee
chalet 'chalet'
chambermaid khadamit el ghorfa
champagne shambania
chance: quite by chance bi sodfa; **no chance!** mafeesh forsa!
change: could you change this into pounds? mumkin teghIyar da lee ginahat?; **I haven't got any change** ma*eesh faka; **can you give me change for a 10 pound note?** mumkin tifukilee *ashara ginay?; **do we have to change (trains)?** eHna lezim nighIyar?; **for a change** litagheer; **you haven't changed the sheets** intee maghIyarteesh; **the place has changed so much** el maken etghIyar khalis; **do you want to change places with me?** *a-Iyiz teghIyar maken ma*ya?; **can I change this for ...?** mumkin aghIyar da lee ...?
changeable (weather) muta'alib
chaos hargalla
chap raagil; **the chap at reception** e-raagil *and el esta*lamat
charge: is there an extra charge? fee ay zeeyada?; **what do you charge?** bitakhud ad ay?; **who's in charge here?** meen e-rIyis hena?
charming badee-a*

chart (diagram) rasma bayanee; (for navigation) khareeta baHaraya
charter flight reHla khasa
chassis 'chassis'
cheap rekhees; **do you have something cheaper?** *andak aya Haga arakhas?
cheat ghash; **I've been cheated** ana etghashayt
check: will you check? mumkin teragaa*?; **will you check the steering?** mumkin tekshif *ala e-driksee-ōn; **will you check the bill?** mumkin teragaa* *alel fatoora; **I've checked it** ana regaa*taha
check (financial) sheek; **will you take a check?** bitekhud sheekat?
check (bill) fatoora; **may I have the check please?** mumkin el fatoora lowsamaHt?
checkbook duhftuhr sheekat
checked (shirt etc) muraba*at
checkers seega
check-in morag*It el kowntuhr
checkroom (for coats etc) amanēt
cheek (on face) khed; **what a cheek!** ya salām!
cheeky (person) bigaH
cheerio (bye-bye) 'bye-bye'
cheers (thank you) shukran; (toast) fee seHetuhk
cheer up farfish kedda
cheese gibna
chef 'chef'
chemist (shop) agzakhenna
cheque sheek; **will you take a cheque?** bitekhud sheekat?
cheque book duhftuhr sheekat
cherry kerez
chess shataruhng
chest (body) sedr
chewing gum leban
chicken ferēkh
chickenpox el gōdaree
child tefl
child minder dāda
child minding service Hadaana
children atfaal
children's playground mal*ab lil

atfaal

children's pool Hammem sibaHa lil atfaal

chilled (*wine*) sa'a*; **it's not properly chilled** da mush sa'a*

chilly bard

chimney madkhana

chin da'uhn (*f*)

china seenee

chips bataatis maHamara (*f*); **potato chips** chips

chocolate shokalaata; **a chocolate bar** shokalaata; **a box of chocolates** *albit shokalaata; **a hot chocolate** kakow

choke (*on car*) howa

cholera 'cholera'

choose ekhtar; **it's hard to choose** min esa*ab tekhtar; **you choose for us** inta tekhtar *alashēnna

chop: a lamb chop reesha dahnee

Christian (*noun, adjective*) miseeHee

Christian name ism

Christmas *ıyeed milad el messeeaH; **merry Christmas** *ıyeed milad sa*yeed

church kineesa; **where is the Protestant church?** fayn el kineesa el brotestaneea?; **where is the Catholic church?** fayn el kineesa el katholeekaya?

cigar sigar

cigarette sigara; **tipped cigarettes** sigara bee filtar; **plain cigarettes** sigara min gheer filtar

cigarette lighter walla*at saggayar

cine-camera kamera sinema'aya

cinema 'cinema'

circle Hala'a; (*in theatre*) balakōn

citadel al*a

citizen: I'm a British citizen ana ingileezee; **I'm an American citizen** ana amrikānee

city medeena

city centre, city center west el balad

claim (*noun: insurance*) ta*oweed

claim form talab ta*oweed

clarify wadaH

classical klassik

classical Arabic logha *arabaya

clean (*adjective*) nedeef; **it's not clean** mush nedeef; **may I have some clean sheets?** mumkin tedeenee milayaat nedeefa?; **our apartment hasn't been cleaned today** sha'a etna matnadafetsh e-naharda; **can you clean this for me?** mumkin tenaduhf da *alashenee?

cleaning solution (*for contact lenses*) maHlool lituhndeef

cleansing cream (*cosmetic*) 'cream' lituhndeef

clear: it's not very clear da mush waadeH; **ok, that's clear** ok da waadeH

clever shaater

cliff hafit e-gabal

climate e-gow

climb: it's a long climb to the top matla* taweel

clinic *ıyeda

cloakroom (*for coats*) amanēt; (*WC*) tawalet

clock sa*at Hayta

close: is it close? da ora-ıyib?; **close to the hotel** ora-ıyib min el fondō'; **close by** mush ba*yeed

close (*verb*) afel; **when do you close?** bite'fil emta?

closed aafil; **they were closed** kan aafil

closet (*cupboard*) dooleb

cloth (*material*) oomash; (*rag*) Hettit oomash

clothes hedoom

clothes line Habl ghaseel

clothes peg, clothespin mashbak

clouds saHab

cloudy maghayim

club nēdee

clubs (*cards*) isbātee

clumsy a*ma

clutch (*car*) debree-aSH; **the clutch is slipping** e-debree-aSH beeyeflet

coach (*long distance bus*) ōtōbees safar

coach party fōg

coach trip reHla seeyaHaya

coast saaHil el baHr; **at the coast** *and

saaHil el baHr
coastguard *amil inkaaz
coat (overcoat etc) baltoo; (jacket) sHakit
coathanger shama*a
cobbler gazmagee
cockroach sorsaar
cocktail 'cocktail'
cocktail bar 'cocktail bar'
cocoa kakow
coconut guz el hind
code: what's the (dialling) code for
...? rakuhm 'code' ... ay?
coffee ahwa; a white coffee, a coffee
with milk ahwa bee laban; a black
coffee ahwa sēda; two coffees,
please itneen ahwa lowsamaHt
coffee pot kanaka
coin *omla
Coke (tm) kakōla
cold (adjective) bard; I'm cold ana
bardēn; I have a cold ana *andee
zookam
cold cream (cosmetic) 'cream'
collapse: he's collapsed oghma *alay
collar ye'a
collar bone *admit e-tarwa'a
colleague saHib; my colleague
saHibee; your colleague saHbak
collect: I've come to collect ... ana
gayt akhud; I collect ... (stamps etc)
ana bagma* ...
collect call this service is not yet possible
from Egypt
college kullaya
collision tuhsadum
colloquial Egyptian Arabic lahga
muhsraya
cologne kulonia
colossus timsēl
colo(u)r lōn; do you have any other
colo(u)rs? *andak alwān tania?
colo(u)r film film milowin
column (of temple etc) *amood
comb (noun) misht
come gay; I come from London ana
gay min 'london'; where do you
come from? inta minayn?; when are
they coming? humma gayeen emta?;
come here ta*ala hena; come with

me ta*ala ma*ya; come back! erga*!;
I'll come back later ana harga*
tanee; come in! itfuhduhl!; he's
coming on very well (improving)
hoowa etHassin awee; come on!
yalla!; do you want to come out this
evening? *a-Iyiz tukhrug elleelādee?;
these two pictures didn't come out
esortayn dōl matel*a-owsh; the
money hasn't come through yet el
feloos lessa magetsh
comfortable (hotel etc) moreeH; it's
not very comfortable mush moreeH
Common Market e-soo' el orōbee
company (firm) shirka; my company
shirkitee
comparison shabeh; there's no
comparison maloosh maseel
compartment (train) saloon
compass bosla
compensation ta*weed
complain ishtaka; I want to
complain about my room *a-Iyiz
ashtikee *an otee
complaint shakwa; I have a
complaint *andee shakwa
complete kaamil; the complete set
ta'm kaamil; it's a complete disaster
museeba kebeera
completely tamaamem
complicated ma*a'd; it's very
complicated da ma*a'd awee
compliment: my compliments to the
chef taHayaatee li 'chef'
comprehensive (insurance) shaamil
compulsory darooree
computer 'computer'
concern: we are very concerned
eHna ala'neen awee
concert Hafla moosikaya
concussion ertigag
condenser (in car) 'condenser'
condition (state) Hala; it's not in very
good condition da mush fee Hala
kwIyissa khalis
conditioner (for hair) balsam
condom kaboot
conductor (on train) komsaree
conference mo'tammuhr

confirm akid; **can you confirm the reservation?** mumkin te-akid el нagz?

confuse: it's very confusing da akhuhr rabka

congratulations! mabrook!

conjunctivitis eltihab eb multaнeema

connection (*in travelling*) wosla

connoisseur khabeer

conscious (*medically*) way*ı-ee

consciousness: he's lost consciousness hoowa fakad wa*ıyoo

constipation imsek

consul 'consul'

consulate konsulaya

contact: how can I contact ...? izzay attessil bee ...?; **I'm trying to contact ... ** ana beнowil attessil bee ...

contact lenses *adessēt laska

contraceptive (*noun*) mene*a lil нaml

contract (*noun*) *a'd

convenient (*time, location*) moola'im; **that's not convenient** da mush moola'im

cook: it's not properly cooked (*is underdone*) da nıyee; **it's beautifully cooked** da mistawee *ız e-talab; **he's a good cook** hoowa tabakh kwıyis

cooker bootagaz

cookie baskaweet

cool (*day, weather*) mooratub

copper naнas aнmar

coppersmith naнas

copt obtee

coptic obtee

coral morgān

coral reef sho*ab morgānee

corduroy ateefa midulla*a

coriander kuzbarra

cork (*in bottle*) fil

corkscrew bareema lifataн el azayz

corn (*on foot*) kuhloo

corner: on the corner (*of street*) *alal nassia; **in the corner** fil rukn; **a corner table** tarabayza lil rukn

cornflakes 'cornflakes'

coronary (*noun*) zabнa suhdraya

correct (*adjective*) saн; **please correct me if I make a mistake** saнaнnee

lowsamaнt

corridor tor'a

corset korsay

cosmetics mawad tagmeel

cost: what does it cost? bikam?

cot (*for baby*) mahd; (*campbed*) sireer khayma

cottage bayt reefee

cotton oton

cotton buds (*for make-up removal etc*) otna tebee

cotton wool otna tebee

couch kanaba

cough (*noun*) кона

cough tablets bastilya

cough medicine dowa кона (*m*)

could: could you ...? mumkin ...?; **could I have ...?** mumkin ...?; **I couldn't ...** ma'adarsh ...

country (*nation*) wotuhn; **in the country** (*countryside*) fil reef

countryside reef

couple (*man and woman*) mitgowzeen; **a couple of boys** waladayn; **a couple of days** yōmayn; *see page 100*

courier morafik seeyaнee

course: of course bitaba*; **of course not** la' taba*an

court (*law*) maнkama; (*tennis*) mal*ab 'tennis'

courtesy bus (*airport to hotel etc*) ōtōbees magēnee

cousin: my cousin (*on mother's side*) (*aunt's daughter*) bint khaltee; (*aunt's son*) ibn khaltee; (*uncle's daughter*) bint khelee; (*uncle's son*) ibn khelee; (*on father's side*) (*aunt's daughter*) bint *amitee; (*aunt's son*) ibn *amitee; (*uncle's daughter*) bint *amee; (*uncle's son*) ibn *amee

cow ba'ra

crab kaaboree-a

cracked: it's cracked (*plate etc*) da mishrookh

cracker (*biscuit*) baskaweet

craftshop maнal maharaat yadawaya

cramp (*in leg etc*) shed *adalee

crankshaft krank

crash нadsa; **there's been a crash** kan

fee Hadsa

crash course (*for learning language etc*) kors mokassif

crash helmet khooza

crawl (*swimming*) krol

crazy mahfoof

cream (*on milk, in cake, for face*) 'cream'

creche (*for babies*) Hadaana

credit card 'credit card'

crib (*baby's cot*) mahd

crisis azma

crisps 'chips'

crockery fokhar

crocodile timseH

crook: he's a crook hoowa nassaab

crossing (*by sea*) *aboor

crossroads takaata* toro'

crosswalk *aboor el mooshaa

crowd nas keteer; (*at football match etc*) mootafaregeen

crowded (*streets, bars*) zaHma

crown (*on tooth*) tag

crucial: it's absolutely crucial darooree giddan giddan

cruise: a cruise down the Nile reHla neelaya

crutches *owkez

cry (*weep*) baka; **don't cry** matebkeesh

cucumber (*small*) kheeyar; (*big*) at-ta

cuisine tuhbkh

cultural sakaafee

cummin kamoon

cup fingal; **a cup of coffee** fingal aHwa

cupboard doolab

cure: have you got something to cure it? *andak Haga te*aleghoo?

curlers roolee

current (*electrical*) tIyar kaharabee; (*in water*) tIyar

curry boohar hindee

curtains settayar

curve (*noun: in road*) malaf

cushion makhada

custom gomruk

Customs gamarek

cut: I've cut myself ana *owart nafsee; **could you cut a little off here?** mumkin te'ta* Hetta min hena?; **we were cut off** (*telephone*) el khat et'ata*; **the engine keeps cutting out** el mator bee'ata*

cutlery fuhdeeyaat

cutlets reesh

cycle: can we cycle there? (*is it far?*) mumkin nerooHa bil *agal?

cylinder (*of car*) 'cylinder'

cylinder-head gasket sHeewān

cynical mustahzi'

Cyprus kobros

cystitis eltihab fil masaana

D

dam sad

damage khoosara; **you've damaged it** inta khasartoo; **it's damaged** khasrit; **there's no damage** mafeesh khoosara

damn! ela*na!

damp (*adjective*) minadee

dance: a local traditional dance ra's sha*bee; **belly-dance** ra's shar'ee; **do you want to dance?** (*to a woman*) *a-Iza tur'ussee?

dancer: he's a good dancer hoowa ra'as Helw

dancing ra's; **we'd like to go dancing** *Izeen nerooH nur'us; **traditional Egyptian dancing** ra's baladee

dandruff eshr

dangerous khatar

dare: I don't dare ana ma*andeesh elgara'a

dark (*adjective*) duhlma; **dark blue** azra' ghēmi'; **when does it get dark?** bitduhlim emta?; **after dark** bil layl
darling Habeebee
dashboard tablō el *arabaya
date: what's the date? e-tareekh ay?; **on what date?** fee tareekh ay?; **can we make a date?** (*romantic, to business partner*) mumkin niratib ma*ad?
dates (*to eat*) balaн
daughter bint; **my daughter** bintee
daughter-in-law miratibnee
dawn (*noun*) fagr; **at dawn** fil fagr
day yum; **the day after** el yum ellee ba*do; **the day before** el yum ellee ablō; **every day** kul yum; **one day** fee yum min el ayem; **can we pay by the day?** mumkin nedfa* bil yōmaya?; **have a good day!** yum sa*yeed!
daylight robbery (*extortionate prices*) ser'a fee *ız e-nahar
day trip reнla yōmaya
dead mayit
deaf atruhsh
deaf-aid sama*a
deal (*business*) suhfuhka; **it's a deal** itafa'na; **will you deal with it?** mumkin ti-oom bee?
dealer (*agent*) taagir
dear (*expensive*) ghelee; **Dear Sir** e-sayid el *azzeez; **Dear Madam** e-sayida el *azzeeza; **Dear Adel** *azzeezee *adel
death mōt
decadent fee tadahworr
December disimbuhr
decent: that's very decent of you da akher zō' minak
decide suhmim; **we haven't decided yet** lessa massuhmimnash; **you decide for us** inta tesuhmim; **it's all decided** kuloo itsuhmim
decision karar
deck (*on ship*) zahr e-safeena
deckchair korsee lil bilasн
declare: I have nothing to declare ma*aya fee нedood el masmooн
decoration (*in room*) dicor

deduct khasm
deep ghaweet; **is it deep?** da ghaweet?
deep-freeze (*noun*) frayzuhr
definitely tab*an; **definitely not** la' tab*an
degree (*university*) shehada gami*ıya; (*temperature*) daraga
dehydrated (*person*) mayit min el *atuhsh; (*medically*) mōgafuhf
delay: the flight was delayed ma*ad e-tıyara etakher
deliberately biluhsd
delicacy: a local delicacy akl maнallee
delicious lazeez
deliver wasal; **will you deliver it?** mumkin tewasaloo?
delivery: is there another mail delivery? fee towzee*-a bareed tanee?
delta deltuh
de luxe luks
denims sнeenz
dent: there's a dent in it fee khabta
dentist garaн asnan
dentures ta'm asnan
deny: he denies it hoowa beeyenkir
deodorant moozeel lireeнet el *ara'
department store maнal kebeer
departure suhfar
departure lounge saalit e-suhfar
depend: it depends yimkin; **it depends on ...** ya-a*timid *ala ...
deposit (*noun: downpayment*) rahan
depressed нazeen
depth *omk
dervish darweesh
description wasf
desert saнara; **in the desert** fi saнara
deserted (*beach, area*) mahgoor
dessert нelw
destination: what's your destination? rıaн fayn?
detergent monozif
detour taнweela
devalued alit imtoo
develop нamuhd; **could you develop these films?** mumkin teнamuhd el

aflam dee?
diabetic (*noun*) muhreed bee sukar
diagram rasm bayānee
dialect lahaga maнalaya
dialling code nimra, 'code'
diamond maas
diamonds (*cards*) deenēree
diaper kafoola
diarrhoea, diarrhea is-hal; **do you have something to stop diarrhoea?** *andak нaga lil is-hal?
diary moofakera
dictionary kaamoos; **an English/ Arabic dictionary** kaamoos ingileezee/*arabee
didn't *see* **not** *and page 112*
die mat; **I'm absolutely dying for a drink** ana mayit min el *atuhsh
diesel (*fuel*) 'diesel'
diet resнeem; **I'm on a diet** ana ba*mil resнeem
difference fer'a; **what's the difference between ...?** ay el fer'a bayn ...?; **I can't tell the difference** mush a'dar afer'a binhoom; **it doesn't make any difference** ma*alesh
different mokhtalif; **they are different** dōl mokhtalifeen; **they are very different** dōl mokhtalifeen awee; **it's different from this one** da mokhtalif *and da; **may we have a different table?** mumkin neghiyar e-tarabayza?; **ah well, that's different** ah, da mokhtalif
difficult sa*b
difficulty sa*ōba; **without any difficulty** min gheer ay sa*ōba; **I'm having difficulties with ...** ana *andee mashēkil ma* ...
digestion haaduhm
dinghy markib sooghıyar
dining car 'buffet'
dining room (*at home*) ōdit suhfra; (*in hotel*) saalit el akl
dinner *asha
dinner jacket sнakit smōkin
dinner party нaflit *asha
dipped headlights e-noor el *adee
dipstick me'yes zayt

direct (*adjective*) mōbēshir; **does it go direct?** bayrooн mōbēshir?
direction etigah; **in which direction is it?** fee ay etigah?; **is it in this direction?** fil e-tigaн da?
directory: telephone directory daleel e-telefonēt
directory enquiries daleel telefonēt
dirt wosekha
dirty mush nedeef
disabled *agiz
disagree: it disagrees with me (*food*) mabit wafi'neesh
disappear ekhtafaa; **it's just disappeared** ekhtafet
disappointed: I was disappointed ana kheb amalee
disappointing: disappointing news akhbar tiza*al; **it was disappointing** kan yiza*al
disaster karsa
discharge (*pus*) khaalees
disc jockey 'disc jockey'
disco 'disco'
disco dancing ra's gharbee
discount (*noun*) takhfeed
disease marad
disgusting (*taste, food etc*) mu'rif
dish (*meal*) akla; (*plate*) tab'a
dishcloth foota
dishwashing liquid se'il lighasl e-saнoon
disinfectant (*noun*) mootaher
disk of film 'disk'
dislocated shoulder kitf mafsool
dispensing chemist sıyeeduhlee
disposable nappies nabee, kafoola tusta*mal mara waнda
distance masēfa; **what's the distance from ... to ...?** el masēfa aday min ... illa ...?; **in the distance** ba*yeed
distilled water mıya ma'atara
distributor (*in car*) asbritēr
disturb aza*ag; **the disco is disturbing us** e-disco za*agna
diversion (*traffic*) taнweela
diving board manat
divorced metuhl'a
dizzy daykh; **I feel dizzy** ana daykh

dizzy spells dōkha
Djibouti sнuhbootee
do: what shall I do? a*mil ay?; **what are you doing tonight?** нata*mil ay elleelādee?; **how do you do it?** bita*miloo izzay?; **will you do it for me?** muмkin te*amiloo *alashēnee?; **who did it?** meen *amaloo?; **the meat's not done** el laнma dee niya; **what do you do?** (job) bitishteghel ay?; **do you have ...?** *andak ...?
docks arsifet el meena
doctor doktor; **he needs a doctor** hoowa meнtag doktor; **can you call a doctor?** muмkin tutlub doktor?
document mustannad
dog kalb
doll *aroosa le*aba
dollar dollar
dome oba
donkey нomar
don't! la'; see not and page 112
door bab
doorman (for apartments etc) bewab; (for hotel) 'doorman'
dosage gura*a
double: double room ōda litneen; **double bed** sireer litneen; **double brandy** dobl brandee; **double r** (in spelling name) 'reh reh'; **it's all double Dutch to me** mish fēhim uhduhk
doubt: I doubt it maftikersh
douche (medical) нo'na
down: get down! enzil!; **he's not down yet** (is in room, bed) hoowa lessa manzelsh; **further down the road** odam shwiya; **I paid 20% down** ana defa*at *ashreen fil maya mō'adam
downmarket (restaurant, hotel) rekhees
downstairs e-dōr e-taнtānee
dozen dasta; **half a dozen** nus dasta
drain (noun: in sink, street) bala*a
draughts (game) seega
draughty: it's rather draughty el howa shedeed shwiya
drawing pin daboos rasm
dreadful (food, holiday, weather etc) mush kwiyis
dream (noun) нelm; **it's like a bad dream** (this trip etc) ziyee kaboos; **sweet dreams** aнlam sa*yeeda
dress (woman's) foostan; **I'll just get dressed** нat-khul albis
dressing (for wound) gheeyar; (for salad) salsa
dressing gown rōb shambar
drink (verb) shirib; **can I get you a drink?** teshrab нaga?; **I don't drink** (alcohol) mabashrabsh; **I must have something to drink** (alcoholic and non-alcoholic) ana lezim ashrab нaga; **a long cool drink** mashroob sa'a*dobl; **may I have a drink of water?** muмkin kubayit miya?; **drink up!** eshrab!; **I had too much to drink** ana shribt keteer
drinkable: is the water drinkable? el miya salнa lil shorb?
drive seh'; **we drove here** gayna bil *arabaya; **I'll drive you home** нawasuhluhk lil bayt bil *arabaya; **do you want to come for a drive?** *a-iyiz lafa fil *arabaya?; **is it a very long drive?** haya masafa too-weela awee?
driver (of car, bus) sawē'
driver's license rukhsit sawē'a
drive shaft *amood el нaraka
driving licence rukhsit sawē'a
drizzle: it's drizzling bitnadda*
drop: just a drop (of drink) shwiya sooghiyara; **I dropped it** ana wa'*atoo; **drop in some time** eb'a *adee
drought gafaf
drown gheri'; **he's drowning** hoowa beyeghera'
drug (medical) dowa (m); (narcotic) mōkhadaraat
drugstore (for medicines) agzakhēnna; (for general goods) maktabba
drunk (adjective) sakraan
dry (adjective) nashif
dry-clean: can I get these dry-cleaned? muмkin tanadaf dōl *ala e-nashif?

dry-cleaner tandeef *ala e-nashif
duck bata
due: when is the bus due? el ōtōbees gay emta?
dumb (can't speak) akhras; (stupid) ghebee
dummy (for baby) bazaza
dune tal
durex (tm) kaboot

during asna'
dust ghoobar
dustbin safeeнet zibella
duty-free (goods) bida*a нora
dynamo 'dynamo'
dynasty osra malakaya; **the tenth dynasty** el osra el malakaya el *ashara
dysentery dusuhnteree-a

E

each kul; **each of them** kul waaнid min hum; **one for each of us** waнda lee kul waaнid; **how much are they each?** bikam el waнda?; **each time** kul mara; **we know each other** eнna ne*aruhf ba*d
ear widnuh
earache: I have earache sup*andee waga* fil widnuh
early badree; **early in the morning** e-subн badree; **it's too early** da badree awee; **a day earlier** yum badree; **half an hour earlier** min nus sa*a; **I need an early night** ana lezim anam badree
early riser: I'm an early riser ana dıman uhsнa badree
earring нala'
earth (soil) teena
earthenware fokhar
east shar'; **to the east** li shar'
Easter *ıyeed el ayama
easy sehl; **easy with the sugar!** shwıya sooghıara!
eat kal; **I want something to eat** *a-ıyiz нaga akolha; **we've already eaten** eнna kalna
eau-de-Cologne kolonya
eccentric shaaz
edible saleн lil akl
efficient (hotel, organization) kofa'
egg bayda

eggplant bitingaana
Egypt masr; **Ancient Egypt** masr el far*onaya
Egyptian (man, adjective) masree; (woman) masraya
Eire irlanda
either ay; **either ... or ...** ay ... ow ...; **I don't like either of them** ana mabнebbish wala waaнid fee hum
elastic (noun) mataat
elastic band astik
Elastoplast (tm) shireet laza'
elbow kuwa*
electric bil kaharaba
electric cooker tabaakh kaharabee
electric fire sakhan kaharaba
electrician kaharaba'ee
electricity kaharaba
electric outlet bareeza
elegant sheek
elevator asuhnsayar
else: something else нaga tanee; **somewhere else** нetta tania; **let's go somewhere else** yalla nerooн нetta tania; **what else?** ay tanee?; **nothing else, thanks** bas kedda, shukran
embarrassed maksoof; **he's embarrassed** hoowa maksoof
embarrassing keesoof
embassy safara
emergency tawari'; **this is an emergency** dee нalit tawari'

emery board mabruhd dawafir kartōn

emotional (*person, time*) *atifee

empty faadee

end (*noun*) nehaya; **the end of the film** nehayit el film; **at the end of the road** fil akhr e-taree'; **when does it end?** bit tekhlas emta?

energetic (*person*) nasheet

energy (*of person*) nashaat

engaged (*to be married*) (*woman*) makhtooba; (*man*) khateb; (*toilet, telephone*) masнghool

engagement ring dibla

engine (*car*) mator; (*diesel*) makenna

engineer mohandis

engineering handessa

engine trouble (*car*) *ıyib fil mator

England ingilterra

English ingileezee; **the English** el ingileez; **I'm English** ana ingileezee; (*woman*) ana ingileezaya; **do you speak English?** bititkallim ingileezee?

Englishman ingileezee

Englishwoman ingileezaya

enjoy: I enjoyed it very much *agabnee awee awee; **enjoy yourself!** matta* nafsak!

enjoyable momte*a

enlargement (*of photo*) takbeer

enormous kebeer awee

enough kifaya; **there's not enough** mafeesh kifaya; **it's not big enough** (*too short*) osıyar awee; (*too small*) sooghıyar awee; **it's not enough** mush kifaya; **thank you, that's enough** shukran, da kifaya

entertainment tasslaya

enthusiastic mutaнamis

entrance (*noun*) madkhel

envelope zarf

epileptic musaab bil sara*

equipment mō*ıdet

eraser asteeka

erotic museer

error ghalat

especially khossoosan

espresso coffee ahwa 'espresso'

essential: it is essential that ... da darooree in ...

estate agent simsar

ethnic (*restaurant, clothes*) baladee

Europe orōba

European orōbee

European plan nus ikaama

even: even the English нatta el ingileez; **even if ...** нatta low ...

evening mise'; **good evening** mise' el kheer; **this evening** el layla dee, elleelādee; **in the evening** bil layl

evening meal *asha

evening dress (*for man*) badla smōkin; (*for woman*) foostan sawareh

eventually akheeran

ever: have you ever been to ...? abadan *omruhk roнt li ...?; **if you ever come to Britain** low gayt lingilterra

every kul; **every day** kul yum

everyone kul waaнid

everything kul наga

everywhere kul нetta

exactly! bizobt!

exam imtaнan

example misēl; **for example** masalan

excellent (*food, hotel*) momtaz; **excellent!** momtaz!

except ma*ada; **except Sunday** ma*ada el нad

exception estesna; **as an exception** kuh estesna

excess baggage *afsh zayid

excessive zayid *ala lezoom; **that's a bit excessive** da zeeyada *ala lezoom

exchange (*verb: money*) нowil; **in exchange** badel *an

exchange rate si-a*r e-taнweel; **what's the exchange rate?** bikam si-a*r e-taнweel?

exciting (*day, holiday*) gameel; (*film*) museer

exclusive (*club, hotel*) li tab'a el *allia

excursion reнla ōsıyara; **is there an excursion to ...?** fee reнla lee ...?

excuse me (*to get past*) lowsamaнt; (*to get attention*) min fadlak; (*pardon?*)

ay?; (*annoyed*) lowsamaнt
exhaust (*on car*) e-shakmaan
exhausted (*tired*) mayit min e-ta*b
exhibition ma*ruhd
exist: does it still exist? lessa
mowgood?
exit khuroog
expect: I expect so *ala ma-azon;
she's expecting haya нamil
expensive ghelee
experience tuhgrōba; **an absolutely
unforgettable experience** tuhgrōba
matitniseesh
experienced khabeer
expert khabeer
expire: it's expired (*passport etc*)
intaha
explain fasuhr; **would you explain
that to me?** mumkin tefasuhr da?
explore estakshif; **I just want to go
and explore** *a-ıyiz arooн estakshif
export (*verb*) suhduhr
exposure meter mi'yes fatнet el

*adessa
express (*mail*) mista*gil; (*train*)
'express', magaree
extra: can we have an extra chair?
mumkin korsee tanee?; **is that
extra?** (*in cost*) da zeeyada?
**extraordinarily: extraordinarily
beautiful** gameel awee awee awee
extraordinary (*very strange*) ghereeb
giddan
extremely awee awee; **that's
extremely expensive** da ghelee awee
awee
extrovert monbuhsit
eye *ın (*f*); **will you keep an eye on
my bags for me?** mumkin tekhellee
baalak min e-shōnuht?
eyebrow нawagib (*f*)
eyebrow pencil alam нawagib
eye drops atra lil *ın
eyeliner koнl
eye shadow zil lil *ıyoon
eye witness shehid

F

fabulous khoorafee
face wish
face mask (*for driving*) nuhdaarit
ghōts
face pack (*cosmetic*) 'mask'
facing: facing the sea ōdam el baнr
fact нa'ee'a
factory masna*
Fahrenheit 'fahrenheit'; *see page 119*
faint: she's fainted ōghma *alayha;
I'm going to faint нıyughma *alaya
fair (*fun-fair*) moolid; (*commercial*)
ma*rad; **it's not fair** da mush *adl;
OK, fair enough mashee khalas
fake ta'leed
fall wi'ya*; **he's had a fall** hoowa
wi'ya*; **he fell off his bike** wi'ya*
min *ala el *agala; **in the fall**

(*autumn*) fil khareef
false muzayif
false teeth ta'm asnan
family *ıayla
family name ism el ıayla
famished: I'm famished ana mayit
min e-gooa*
famous mashhoor
fan (*mechanical, hand-held*) marawaнa;
(*football etc*) mushaga*a
fan belt sayuhr el marawaнa
fancy mo*gabee; **he fancies you**
hoowa mo*gab beekee
fantastic modhish
far ba*yeed; **is it far?** da ba*yeed?;
how far is it to ...? el masefa dee ay
lee ...?; **as far as I'm concerned**
binesbaalee

fare ōgra; **what's the fare to ...?** el ōgra kam lee ...?

farm *azba

farther ab*ad; **farther than ...** ab*ad min ...

fashion (*in clothes etc*) mōda

fashionable akher mōda

fast saree-a*; **not so fast** mush bisora*a

fast (*noun*) seeyaam; **are you fasting?** inta sɪyim?

fastener (*zip*) sosta

faster/fastest asra*

fat (*person*) tekheen; (*on meat*) simeen

father ab; **my father** abooya

father-in-law (*father of wife*) aboo el madam; (*fatheer of husband*) aboo gooz

fathom arar

fattening disim

faucet Hanafaya

fault zamb; **it was my fault** da zambee ana; **it's not my fault** mush zambee ana

faulty (*equipment*) fee *ɪyib

favo(u)rite mazeg; **that's my favo(u)rite** da mazēgee

fawn (*colour*) bonee asfar fete*H

February fibrɪuhr

fed up: I'm fed up ana zah'en; **I'm fed up with ...** ana zah'en min ...

feeding bottle ezazzit reeda*a

feel: I feel hot ana Haraan; **I feel cold** ana sa'*an; **I feel like a drink** *a-ɪyiz ashrab Haga; **I don't feel like it** (*doing something*) maleesh mazeg; (*food, drink*) maleesh nifs; **how are you feeling today?** izzay saHetuhk e-naharda?; **I'm feeling a lot better** ana Hassis bitaHassun

fence soor

fender (*of car*) ekseedaam

ferry ma*daya; **what time's the last ferry?** emta akher ma*daya?

festival mahragaan

fetch gēb; **I'll go and fetch it** ana HarooH ageeboo; **will you come and fetch me?** mumkin teegee tekhudnee?

fever Humaa

feverish: I'm feeling feverish ana Hassis bee sukhunaya

few shwɪya; **only a few** shwɪya bas; **a few minutes** da'ay'; **he's had a good few** (*to drink*) shirib keteer

fiancé: my fiancé khateebee

fiancée: my fiancée khatibtee

fiasco: what a fiasco! karsa!

field ghayt

fifty-fifty nus-nus

fight (*noun*) khina'a

figs teen

figure (*of person*) kasm; (*number*) *adad; **I have to watch my figure** ana lezim aHafiz *ala kasmee

fill mala; **fill her up please** imlaha lowsamaHt; **will you help me fill out this form?** mumkin tesa*adnee amla e-namoozag da?

fillet shareeHa

filling (*in tooth*) Hashw; **it's very filling** (*food*) da yishaba* awee

filling station maHattit benzeen

film (*in cinema, for camera*) film; **do you have this type of film?** *andak nooa* el film da?; **16mm film** film sittaashar millee; **35mm film** film khamsa wi talaateen millee

filter (*for camera, coffee*) filtuhr

filter-tipped bi filtuhr

filthy (*room etc*) wisikh

find le'eh; **I can't find it** mush le'eeh; **if you find it** low le'it-hoo; **I've found a ...** ana le'eet ...

fine kwɪyis; **that's fine** da kwɪyis; **I'm fine** ana kwɪyis; **it's fine weather** gow gameel; **how are you? — fine thanks** izzayak? — kwɪyis; **a 30 pound fine** talaateen ginay ghuhrama

finger sooba*

fingernail dofr e-sooba*

finish khalas; **I haven't finished** lessa makhalastish; **when I've finished** lama khalas; **when does it finish?** bitakhlas emta?; **finish off your drink** khalas mashroobuhk

fire narr (*f*); **fire!** (*i.e. something's on*

fire) Haree'a!; **may we light a fire here?** mumkin noowala* narr hena?; **it's on fire** moowala*a; **it's not firing properly** (*car*) el mator bee'uhta*

fire alarm garuhs inzar

fire brigade, fire department el mataafee

fire escape makhruhg

fire extinguisher tafiet Haree'a

firm (*company*) shirka; **my firm** shirkitee

first owel; **I was first** ana kunt el owel; **at first** awalan; **this is the first time** dee owel mara

first aid issa*af awalee

first aid kit shantit iss*af awalee

first class (*travel etc*) darga oola

first name ism

fish (*noun*) samak

fisherman sayad samak

fishing sayid e-samak

fishing boat markib sayid

fishing net shabakit sayid samak

fishing rod sinara

fishing tackle *idit sayid samak

fishing village kareeyit sayid samak

fit (*healthy*) layi'; **I'm not very fit** ma*ndeesh lee ye'a; **he's a keep fit fanatic** hoowa mazegoo el leeye'a; **it doesn't fit** mush monasib

fix: can you fix it? mumkin tessalHoo?; **let's fix a time** yalla niHadid ma*ad; **it's all fixed up** kuloo tamem; **I'm in a bit of a fix** ana fee mowkif moHrig

fizzy fowarr

fizzy drink mashroob fowarr

flab (*on body*) simeen

flag *alam

flannel (*face*) foota; (*fabric*) fanilla

flash (*for camera*) 'flash'

flashlight battaraya

flashy (*clothes etc*) iyim

flat (*adjective*) moosataH; **this beer is flat** el beera dee mush kwiyissa; **I've got a flat tyre/tire** el kawetsh nayim; (*apartment*) sha'a

flatterer monafi'

flatware (*cutlery*) fuhdeeyaat; (*crockery*)

fokhar

flavo(u)r ta*am

flea barghoot

flea bite arsit barghoot

flea powder budrit barragheet

flexible (*material, arrangements*) marin

flies (*on trousers*) fatHet el bantalon

flight tiyara

flippers za*anif

flirt dalēl

float *awēma

flood fiadaan

floor (*of room*) ard (*f*); **on the floor** *alel ard; **on the second floor** (*UK*) fidor e-taalit; (*US*) fidor e-tanee

floorshow *ard

flop (*failure*) fashal

florist maHal zuhor

flour di'ee'

flower zahra

flu infilwenza

fluent tuhlee'; **he speaks fluent Arabic** hoowa bikellim *arabee beetuhla'a

fly (*verb*) tarr; **can we fly there?** mumkin nerooH bi tiyara?

fly (*insect*) dibana

fly spray bakhakhit diban

fog shabora; **it's foggy** e-gow shabora

fog lights noor li shabora

folk dancing ra's folkloree

folk music mooseeka sha*baya; (*in Upper Egypt*) mooseeka suhi-eedee

follow tebe*a; **follow me** tabe*anee

fond: I'm quite fond of ... ana moghruhm bee ...

food akl; **the food's excellent** el akl momtaz

food poisoning tassamum

food store maHal bee'ala

fool ghebee

foolish ghebee

foot rigl; **on foot** *ala e-riglayn; *see page 117*

football (*game, ball*) kora kuhduhm

for *alashēn; **is that for me?** da *alashēnee?; **what's this for?** da *alashēn ay?; **for two days** limodit yoomayn; **I've been here for a week**

ana ba'alee hena isboo*a; **a bus for ... ** ōtōbees lee ...

forbidden mamnoo-a* (*strictly and religiously*) Haraam; **is it forbidden?** da Haraam?

forehead oora

foreign agnabee

foreigner (*man*) agnabee; (*woman*) agnabaya

foreign exchange (*money*) taHweel *omla

forget nessee; **I forget, I've forgotten** niseet; **don't forget** matinsash

fork (*for eating*) shoka; (*in road*) tafare*a

form (*in hotel, to fill out*) namoozag

formal (*dress*) Heshma; (*person*) dōghree; (*language*) rasmaya

fortnight isboo*ayn

fortress al*a

fortunately lay Hosn el Haz

fortune-teller *araf

forward: could you forward my mail? mumkin teba*t gowabatee *ala el *ɪnwān e-gedeed?

forwarding address el *ɪnwān e-gedeed

foundation cream 'cream' Himaya

fountain (*ornamental*) nafora; (*for drinking*) Hanafaya

foyer (*of hotel, theatre*) saala

fracture (*noun*) sha'

fractured skull gomgomma mash'oo'a

fragile sahl el kasr

frame (*for picture*) biroo-ez

France faransa

fraud nasb

free (*at liberty*) Hohr; (*costing nothing*) bi balash; **admission free** e-dikhool bi balash

freezer frayzuhr

freezing cold bard awee awee

French (*adjective, language*) fransaawee

French fries batates maHamara

frequent *alatool

fresh (*weather, breeze*) mon*esh; (*fruit etc*) taaza; (*cheeky*) sehee; **don't get fresh with me** mat-Howelsh ma*aya

fresh orange juice *aseer bortooa'n taaza

friction tape shireet *ɪzil

Friday el gom*a

fridge talaga

fried egg bayda ma'laya

friend saHib

friendly Hebbee

frog dovd*a

from min; **I'm from London** ana min 'london'; **from here to the sea** min hena lil baHr; **the next boat from ...** el markib e-gay min ...; **as from Tuesday** min yum e-talaat

front wag-ha; **in front** ōdam; **in front of us** ōdamna; **at the front** fil mō'dimma

frozen migammid; **frozen food** akl migammid

fruit fawaki

fruit juice *aseer fawaki

fruit salad salatit fawaki

frustrating moHIyar; **it's very frustrating** moHIyar awee

fry (*vegetables*) Hamar; (*fish*) ala; **nothing fried** wala Haga ma'laya

frying pan taasa

full malyan; **it's full of ...** malyan bee ...; **I'm full** (*eating*) ana shaba*an

full-board ikaama kamla

fun mōt*a; **it's fun** da mōt*a; **it was great fun** kan momte*a; **just for fun** li taslaya; **have fun** mata* nafsak

funeral ganaza

funny (*strange*) ghereeb; (*amusing*) fookehee

furniture asses

further aba*d; **2 kilometres further** ba*d itneen kiloomitr; **further down the road** ōdam shwɪya

fuse: the lights have fused e-noor darab

fuse wire silk musahir

future moost'abil; **in future** fil moost'abil

G

gale *asifa
gallon see page 119
gallstones el Haswa e-suhfra
gamble aamir; I don't gamble ana maleesh fil ōmar
game le*aba
games room saalit el le*ab
garage (petrol) maHattit benzeen; (repair) warshit *arabeeyaat; (for parking) mow'af *arabeeyaat
garbage zibella
garden goonayna
garlic tōm
gas ghez; (gasoline) benzeen
gas cylinder (for Calor gas) anboobit bootagaz
gasket takhsheena
gas pedal dawāset el benzeen
gas station maHattit benzeen
gas tank khazan benzeen
gastroenteritis eltihab fil masareen
gate (also at airport) bewābba
gauge mi'yes
gay (homosexual) khawal
gear tirs; the gears keep sticking e-tuhroos bititzini' ma*a ba*daha
gearbox sandoo' e-tuhroos; I have gearbox trouble fee *Iyib fee sandoo' e-tuhroos
gear lever, gear shift *asIyit el fitis
gekko seHlaya
general delivery you have a post box number: sandoo' bareed rakuhm
generous kareem; that's very generous of you da karuhm kebeer minak
gentleman (man) moHtaram; that gentleman over there el akh el moHtaram ellee hinak; he's such a gentleman hoowa moHtaram giddan
gents (toilet) tawalet rigālee

genuine Ha'ee'ee
German measles el Hazba el almanaya
Germany almanya
get: have you got ...? (in a shop) *andak ...?, fee ...?; (said to a woman) *andik ...?; have you got my address? ma*ak *Inwānee?; how do I get to ...? izzay arooH lil ...?; where do I get it from? *ageeboo minayn?; can I get you a drink? teshrab ay?; will you get it for me? mumkin tigibhoolee?; when do we get there? Hanoosal emta?; I've got to ... ana lezim ...; I've got to go ana lezim amshee; where do I get off? anzil fayn?; it's difficult to get to sa*ab el wisool lee; when I get up (in morning) lama asHa
ghastly fazee-a*
ghost shabaH
giddy dayekh; it makes me giddy bekhaleenee adōkh
gift hidaya
gigantic dakhm
gin sHin; a gin and tonic sHin wee tonik
girl bint
girlfriend saHibitee
give edda; will you give me ...? mumkin teddeenee ...?; I'll give you one pound Hadeeluk ginay; I gave it to him ana eddit-hooloo; will you give it back? mumkin terega*oo?; would you give this to ...? mumkin teddee da lee ...?
glad mabsoot
glamorous (woman) fatenna
gland ghoda
glandular fever Homa fil ghodad
glass (material) eezez; (for drinking)

koobaya; **a glass of water** koobayit mɪya

glasses (*spectacles*) nuhdara

gloves gawantee

glue (*noun*) samgh

gnat namoosa

go raн; **we want to go to ...** *ɪzeen nerooн lee ...; **I'm going there tomorrow** ana rɪaн hinak bukra; **when does it go?** (*bus etc*) beeyetla* emta?; **where are you going?** inta rɪaн fayn?; **let's go** yalla nimshee; **he's gone** hoowa mishee; **it's all gone** khalaas; **I went there yesterday** ana roнt hinak imbarraн; **go away!** imshee!; **it's gone off** (*milk etc*) fēhsid; **we're going out tonight** eнna khargeen e-layla dee; **do you want to go out tonight?** *a-ɪyiz tukhrug e-layla dee?; **has the price gone up?** e-tamen zād?

goal (*sport*) gōn

goat me*aza

goat's cheese gibnit m*ɪ-eez

God allah; **God willing** inshah' allah

god illah

goddess illaha

gold dahab

golf 'golf'

golf clubs *asɪyit el golf

golf course malab el golf

good kwɪyis; **good!** kwɪyis!; **that's no good** da mush kwɪyis; **good heavens!** allahoo akbar!

goodbye ma*asalemma

good-looking (*man*) damoo khafeef; (*woman*) damaha khafeef

gooey (*food etc*) milaza' wimsuhkar

goose wizza

gorgeous gameel

government нōkooma

gradually shwɪya shwɪya

grammar *alm e-naнw

gram(me) giraam; *see page 117*

granddaughter нafeeda

grandfather gid

grandmother gidda

grandson нafeed

granny nayna

grapefruit graybfroot

grapefruit juice *aseer graybfroot

grapes *ɪnab; (*small, seedless*) *ɪnab banātee; (*large, sweet, brown*) *ɪnab fayoomee

grass (*on lawn, drug*) нasheesh

grateful mootshēkir; **I'm very grateful to you** ana mootshēkir giddan

gravy dima*a

gray roomaadee

grease (*for car*) shaнm; (*on food*) dehn

greasy (*food*) dehnee

great *azeem; **that's great!** da *azeem!

Great Britain ingilterra

Greece el yoonan

greedy tama*

green akhdar

greengrocer khōdaree

grey roomaadee

grilled mashwee

gristle (*on meat*) ar'oosha

grocer ba'ēl

ground ard (*f*); **on the ground** *alel ard; **on the ground floor** fil dōhr el ardee

ground beef laнma mafrooma

group magmoo*a

group insurance ta'meen

group leader rɪyis

guarantee (*noun*) damaan; **is it guaranteed?** da *alay damaan?

guardian (*of child*) walay el umr

guest dayif

guesthouse benseeyōn

guest room ōdit e-zoo-war

guide (*noun*) morshid

guidebook daleel siyāнee

guilty mōgrim

guitar 'guitar'

Gulf States el khaleeg el *arabee

gum lessa; (*chewing gum*) liban

gun bundoo'aya

gymnasium saalit e-reeyada el badanaya

gyn(a)ecologist akhissaa'ee uhmraad nissa

gypsum gibs

H

hair sha*r
hairbrush forshit sha*r
haircut uhs e-sha*r; **just an ordinary haircut please** uhs baseet lowsamaнt
hairdresser kowafayar
hairdryer eksishwar
hair gel 'gel' li sha*r
hair grip bensit sha*r; (*with fancy decoration*) tooka
hair lacquer lakay lil sha*r
hair style: have you got a catalogue of hairstyles? *andik 'catalogue'?
half nus; **half an hour** nus sa*a; **half a litre/liter** nus litr; **half as much** nusi da; **half as much again** nusi da kamem
halfway: halfway to Cairo fee nus e-sikka lil kaheera
hamburger 'hamburger'
hammer (*noun*) shakoosh
hand eed; **hands** eedayn; **will you give me a hand?** mumkin tesa*adnee?
handbag shantit eed
hand baggage shanta
handbrake faraamil eed
handkerchief mandeel
handle (*noun*) okra; **will you handle it?** mumkin te*amiloo?
hand luggage shanta
handmade sōna* yadawee
handsome damoo khafeef
hanger (*for clothes*) shama*a
hangover suda*; **I've got a terrible hangover** *andee suda* shedeed
happen hassal; **how did it happen?** нassal izzay?; **what's happening?** ay ellee beyaнsal?; **it won't happen again** mush нate-aнsal tanee
happy mabsoot; **we're not happy with the room** eнna mush

mo*agabeen bil ōda
harbo(u)r meena
hard gamid; (*difficult*) sa*b
hard-boiled egg bayda masloo-a awee
hardly (*with difficulty*) biso*ooba; **hardly ever** nadir; **there's hardly any left** mafeesh keteer
hardware store maнal adawet manzilaya
harem нareem
harm (*noun*) azaya
hassle: it's too much hassle kuloo mata*ıb; **a hassle-free trip** reнla bidoon mata*ıb
hat ta'aya
hate: I hate ... ana bakra ...
have: do you have ...? (*in a shop etc*) *andak ...?, fee ...?; (*said to a woman*) *andik ...?; **do you have any money?** ma*ak feloos?; **can I have ...?** mumkin ...?; **can I have some water?** mumkin shwıyit mıya?; **I have ...** *andee ...; **I don't have ...** ma*andeesh ...; **can we have breakfast in our room?** mumkin neftar fee ōditna?; **have another medeeduhk**; **I have to leave early** ana lezim amshee badree; **do I have to ...?** ana lezim ...?; **do we have to ...?** eнna lezim ...?; *see page 114*
hay fever zookam rabee*ı
he hoowa; **is he here?** hoowa hena?; **where does he live?** hoowa sekin fayn?; *see page 106*
head ras (*f*); **we're heading for Aswan** eнna rıнeen aswaan
headache suda*
headgear kiswuh li ras
headlights e-noor el amāmee
headphones sama*at
headscarf asharb

headsquare (*large traditional*) talfeeнa
head waiter ra'ees el garsonat
head wind ree-aн *aksaya
health seнa; **your health!** fiseнuhtuhk!
healthy (*person, food, climate*) seнee
hear simea*; **can you hear me?** te'dar tisma*nee?; **I can't hear you** ana mush sam*ak; **I've heard about it** seema*t *anha
hearing aid sama*it widn
heart alb
heart attack zabнa sadraya
hearts (*cards*) kōba
heat нarara; **not in this heat!** mush fil нarr da!
heater (*in car*) sakhen
heating tadfi'a
heat rash нamoneel
heat stroke darbit shams
heatwave mogit нarr
heavy ti'eel
hectic lakhbuhtta
heel (*of foot, of shoe*) ka*b; **could you put new heels on these?** mumkin terakibluhum ka*b gedeed?
heelbar tuhsleeyeн gizzam
height *ıloo
helicopter 'helicopter'
hell: oh hell! e-la*na!; **go to hell!** rooн fi daheeya!
hello ahlan; (*in surprise*) mish ma*ool!; (*on phone*) allō
helmet (*for motorcycle*) khooza
help (*verb*) seh*ıd; **can you help me?** mumkin tesa*ıdnee?; **thanks for your help** shukran; **help!** нa'oonee!
helpful: he was very helpful hoowa kan mufeed awee; **that's helpful** da mufeed awee
helping: can I have another helping? mumkin tanee?
henna нenna
hepatitis eltihab fil kibd
her: I don't know her ana ma*rafhaash; **will you send it to her?** mumkin teb*at-helha?; **it's her** dee haya; **with her** ma*aha; **for her** *alashēnha: **her house** bayt-ha; **her**

husband goozha; **that's her suitcase** dee shantit-ha; *see pages 105, 106*
herbs a*asheb
here hena; **here you are** (*giving something*) itfuhduhl; **here he comes** hoowa gay
hers bita*ha; **that's hers** da bita*ha; *see page 108*
hey! (*to a man*) inta!; (*to a woman*) intee!
hi! 'hi!'
hibiscus karkaday
hiccups zooghotta
hide istakhaba
hideous fazee-a*
hieroglyphics hıroghleefaya
high *alee
highbeam e-noor el *alee
highchair korsee *alee
highway taree' sareeya*
hill matla*; **it's further up the hill** shwıya fo' el matla*
hillside gamb el matla*
hilly kuloo matale-a*
him: I don't know him ana ma*rafhoosh; **will you send it to him?** mumkin teb*at-hooloo; **it's him** da hoowa; **with him** ma*ah; **for him** *alashēnoo; *see page 106*
hip hunsh
hire uhguhr; **can I hire a car?** mumkin a-uhguhr *arabaya?; **do you hire them out?** inta bituhguhrhum?
his: his house baytoo; **his wife** miraatoo; **it's his drink** da mashrooboo; **it's his** da bita*oo; *see pages 105, 108*
history tareekh; **the history of the Pharaohs** tareekh el fara*ana
hit darab; **he hit me** hoowa darabnee; **I hit my head** ana khabat rasee
hitch: is there a hitch? fee нaga?
hit record oghnaya mush-hora
hole khorum
holiday agēzza; **I'm on holiday** ana fi agēzza
Holland hollanda
home bayt; **at home** (*in my house etc*)

fil bayt; (*in my country*) fi baladee; **I
go home tomorrow** ana marowaн
bukra
home address *ınwān el bayt
homemade baytee; (*made in the shop
etc*) maнallee
homesick: I'm homesick ana mushte'
arga* lee baladee
honest ameen
honestly? на'ee?
honey *asal naнl
honeymoon shahr el *asal; **we are on
our honeymoon** eнna fi shahr el
*asal
hood (*of car*) kaboot
hoover (*tm*) maknassa bil kaharaba
hope amal; **I hope so** atmana haza; **I
hope not** matmanash
horn (*of car*) kalaks; (*of animal*) arn
horrible mor*ıb
hors d'oeuvre mazzah
horse hossaan
horse riding rikoob el kheel
hose (*for car radiator*) кhartum mıya
hospital mustashfa
hospitality karam; **thank you for
your hospitality** shukran *ala
karamak
hostel mo*askuhr shebab
hot sukhn; (*curry etc*) нamee; **I'm
hot** ana нaraan; **something hot
to eat** нaga sukhna akulha; **it's
so hot today** e-gow нarr awee

e-naharda
hotel fondō'; **at my hotel** fil fondō'
hotel clerk (*receptionist*) moo-wazuhf
isti'bel
hotplate (*on cooker*) 'hotplate'
hour sa*a; **on the hour** kul sa*a
house bayt
housewife rabit bayt
house wine nebeez maнallee
how izzay; **how many?** ad'ay?; **how
much?** bikam?; **how often?** kul
ad'ay?; **how are you?** (*to a man*)
izzayak?; (*to a woman*) izzayik?; **how
do you do?** (*to a man*) izzayak?; (*to a
woman*) izzayik?; **how about a beer?**
teshrab beera?; **how nice!** fekra
momtaza!; **would you show me how
to?** mumkin tewarreenee?
humid moratuhb
humidity rotooba
**humo(u)r: where's your sense of
humo(u)r?** fayn soobak el fookehee?
hundredweight *see page 118*
hungry: I'm hungry ana ga*an; **I'm
not hungry** ana mush ga*an
hurry: I'm in a hurry ana mista*gil;
hurry up! yalla bisora*a!; **there's no
hurry** *ala mahlak
hurt: it hurts bitooga*; **my back
hurts** dahree beeyooga*nee
husband zog; **my husband** goozee
hydro-electric кahroomē'ee
hydrofoil luhnsh muhtaat, 'hydrofoil'

I

I ana; **I am English** (*man*) ana
ingileezee; (*woman*) ana ingileezaya;
I live in Manchester ana *ı-ish
fee 'manchester'; *see page 106*
ice talg; **with ice** bi talg; **with ice and
lemon** bi talg wi lamoon
ice cream 'ice cream', sнelatee
ice-cream cone 'ice cream' fee

baskoot
ice lolly lollee-uhb
idea fikra; **good idea!** fikra kwıyissa!
ideal (*solution, time*) missēlee
identity papers owra'a shakhsaya
idiot ghebee
idyllic gazāb
if low; **if you could** low te'dar; **if not**

low la'a
ignition marsh
ill *ɪyēn; **I feel ill** ana *ɪyēn
illegal gheer shar*ɪ
illegible mush waadeн
illness marad
imitation (*leather etc*) te'leed
immediately нālan
immigration hegra
import (*verb*) estowrid
important mōhim; **it's very important** da mōhim awee; **it's not important** da mush mōhim
impossible mustaнeel
impressive mo'assir
improve: it's improving bitit-нassin; **I want to improve my Arabic** ana *a-ɪyiz aнassin el *arabee bita*ee
improvement taнseen
in fee; **in my room** fee ōtee; **in the town centre** fee west el balad; **in Cairo** fil kaheera; **in London** fee 'london'; **in one hour's time** fee mōdit sa*a; **in August** fee aghostos; **in English** bil ingileezee; **in Arabic** bil *arabee; **is he in?** hoowa mowgood?
inch boosa; *see page 117*
include: is that included in the price? da maнsoob fi se*ar?
incompetent khayb
inconvenient mush moola'im
increase (*noun*) zeeyāda
incredible (*very good, amazing*) mōdhish
indecent aleel el adab
independent нorr
India el hind
Indian (*man, adjective*) hindee; (*woman*) hindaya
Indian Ocean el mōнeet el hindee
indicator (*on car*) noor eeshaara
indigestion soo' hadam
indoor pool нammem sibaнa shitwee
indoors gowa
industry sina*a
inefficient mush kwɪyis
infection *adwa
infectious mo*adee

inflammation eltihab
inflation tadakhum
informal (*clothes, occasion, meeting*) mush rasmee
information ma*lōmat
information desk esta*lamat
information office maktab el esta*lamat
injection нo'na
injured insaab; **she's been injured** haya insaabit
injury eesaaba
innocent baree'a
inquisitive fidoolee
insect нashara
insect bite arsit нashara
insecticide moobeed lil нasharaat
insect repellent taarid lil нasharaat
inside: inside the tent fil khayma; **let's sit inside** yalla no'a*d gowa
insincere mush ameen
insist: I insist ana muser
insomnia aruhk
instant coffee 'nescafe'
instead badal; **I'll have that one instead** ana нekhud da aнsen; **instead of ...** badal min ...; **can we go to Luxor instead of Aswan?** mumkin nerooн lu'sor badal min aswaan?
insulating tape shireet *ɪzil
insulin 'insulin'
insult (*noun*) eehāna
insurance ta'meen; **write your insurance company here** ekitb ism shirkit ta'meenak hena
insurance policy boleesit ta'meen
intellectual (*noun*) musakuhf
intelligent zakee
intentional: it wasn't intentional makensh ma'sood
interest: places of interest amakin lil mota*a
interested: I'm very interested in ... ana mohtam awee bee ...
interesting mumtea*; **that's very interesting** da mumtea* awee
international *alemmee
international driving licence rokhsit

sawē'a dowlaya
interpret targim; **would you interpret?** mumkin tetergim?
interpreter motergim
intersection (*crossroads*) ta'aata* turo'
interval (*during play etc*) estiraHa
into lil; **I'm not into that** (*don't like*)
ana mabaHebboosh
introduce: may I introduce ...?
mumkin a*rafuhk ...?
introvert montaawee
invalid (*not legal*) baatil; (*noun: person*)
*Iyēn
invalid chair korsee lil *agazuh
invitation (*general*) da*wa; (*for meal*)
*Izooma; **thank you for the invitation** shukran *ala e-da*wa; **thank
you for the dinner invitation**
shukran *ala el *Izooma
invite da*a; **can I invite you out?**
mumkin a*zimak bara?
**involved: I don't want to get in-
volved in it** ana mush *a-Iyiz
adakhil
iodine sabghityood
Iran iraan
Iranian (*man, adjective*) iraanee;
(*woman*) iraanaya

Iraq el *Ira'
Iraqi *Ira'ee
Ireland irlanda
Irish irlandee
Irishman irlandee
Irishwoman irlandaya
iron (*material*) Hadeed; (*for clothes*)
makwa; **can you iron these for me?**
mumkin tekwee dōl *alashēnee?
ironmonger maHal adawet manzillaya
irrigation e-rI
is *see page 113*
Islam el islam
island gezeera
isolated ma*zool
Israel isra-eel
Israeli isra-eelee
it (*for masculine nouns*) da; (*for feminine
nouns*) dee; **is it ...?** da/dee?; **where
is it?** fayn da/dee?; **it's her** dee
haya; **it was ...** kan ...; **that's just it**
(*just the problem*) dee el mushkilla;
that's it (*that's right*) saH!; *see page
106*
Italy ituhlya
itch: it itches bitakulnee
itinerary khat e-reHla

J

jack (*for car*) sHak; (*cards*) walad
jacket sHakit
jam (*preserve*) mirabuh; **apricot jam**
mirabit mishmish; **a traffic jam**
zaHmit maroor; **I jammed on the
brakes** dosta *ala el faraamil
January yanaayuhr
jaundice marad e-suhfruh
jasmine yasmeen
jaw fak
jazz mooseeka el sHaz
jealous ghIyoor; **he's jealous** hoowa
ghIyoor

jeans sHeenz
jellyfish samak hoolāmee
jerboa far el ghayit
Jerusalem el ods
jetty raseef
Jew (*man, adjective*) yahoodee; (*woman*)
yahoodaya
jewel(le)ry moogowharaat
Jewish yahoodee
jiffy: just a jiffy estanna shwiya
job shoghl; **just the job!** (*just right*) da
tamam; **it's a good job you told me!**
kwIyis ellee inta oltillee

jog: I'm going for a jog ana гιaн
agree
jogging garee-y
join: I'd like to join ana *a-ιyiz
eltaнuh'; **can I join you?** (go with)
mumkin arooн ma*ak; (sit with)
mumkin a*od ma*ak?; **do you want
to join us?** (go with) *a-ιyiz teegee
ma*ana?; (sit with) *a-ιyiz to'a*od
ma*ana?
joint (in body) mufasalla; (to smoke)
нasheesh
joke nokta; **you've got to be joking!**
inta lezim bitnakit!; **it's no joke** dee
mush nokta
joker 'joker'
jolly: it was jolly good kan нelw
awee; **jolly good!** нelw awee!
Jordan el ordun
Jordanian (man, adjective) ordōnee;
(woman) ordōnaya
journey reнla; **have a good journey!**
reнla sa*ιeeda!; **safe journey!**

tewoosal bi salemma!
jug abree'; **a jug of water** shafsha'
mιya
July yulya
jump nuht; **you made me jump**
inta khadetnee; **jump in!** (to car)
erkab!
jumper bullōvuhr
jump leads, jumper cables kablēt
junction takaata*
June yoonya
junior: Mr Ahmed junior el ōstez
ahmed el sooghιyar
junk (rubbish) zibella
just: just one waaнid bas; **just me**
ana bas; **just for me** laya ana bas;
just a little shwιya sooghιyara; **just
here** bas hena; **not just now** mush
delwa'tee; **that's just right** da taman;
it's just as good da yenfa*; **he was
here just now** hoowa kan hena
delwa'tee; **I've only just arrived** ana
lessa waasil delwa'tee

K

kebab kebab
keen: I'm not keen maleesh mazeg
keep: can I keep it? mumkin
akhaleeh?; **please keep it** khalee
ma*ak; **keep the change** khalee el
be'ee; **will it keep?** (food) нat*ι-
eesh?; **it's keeping me awake**
mikhaleenee saaнee; **it keeps on
breaking** dιman tetkessir; **I can't
keep anything down** (food) ana
batrush aya нaga
kerb raseef
kerosene gas
ketchup 'ketchup'
kettle baraad
key muftaн
kid: the kids el *ιyēl; **I'm not
kidding** ana mush banakit

kidneys (body) killa; (food) kallawee
kill atal
kilo keeloo; see page 118
kilometre, kilometer keeloomitr; see
page 117
kind: that's very kind da zo' minak;
this kind of ... nōa* el ...; **I don't
like this kind of food** ana
mabaнebbish nōa* el akl da
king malik; (cards) shayib
kiosk koshk
kiss (noun) boosa; (verb) bes
kitchen mutbukh
kitchenette mutbukh sooghιyar
Kleenex (tm) kliniks
knee rukba
kneecap saboonit e-rukba
knickers kulotēt нareemee

knife sikeena
knitting (act, material) tereekō
knitting needles ebar tereekō
knock: there's a knocking noise from the engine fee khabuht fil mator; he's had a knock on the head hoowa etkhabuht *ala deemeghoo; he's been knocked over hoowa we'a*
knot (in rope) *a'oda
know (somebody, something) *arif; I don't know ma*arafsh; do you know a good restaurant? te*araf mat*am kwıyiz?; who knows? ma*arafsh; I didn't know that ana ma*areftish da; I don't know him ana ma*arafoosh
Koran kur'aan
Kuwait koowayt
Kuwaiti (man, adjective) koowaytee; (woman) koowaytaya

L

label tikit
laces (for shoes) roobaat gazma
lacquer (for hair) lakay
ladies (room) tawalet
lady madam; ladies and gentlemen! sayidatee saadatee!
lager stella (tm)
lake birka
lamb (meat) daanee; (animal) oozee
lamp lamba
lamppost *amood e-noor
lampshade abasHora
land (not sea) ard (f); when does the plane land? e-tıyara Hatewoosal emta?
lane (small street) Haara; (a country lane) zira*ee
language logha
language course kors logha
large kebeer
laryngitis eltihab fil Huhngara
last akheer; last year e-sana ellee fatit; last Wednesday el arba* ellee fat; last week el isboo-a* ellee fat; last night lilt-imbarraH; when's the last bus? akheer ōtōbees emta?; one last drink akheer waaHid; when were you last in London? emta kunt akheer mara fi 'london'?; at last! akheeran!; how long does it last? bitakhud ad ay?
last name ism el *ıla
late mitaakhuhr; sorry I'm late asif *ala takheer; don't be late matitakharsh; the bus was late el ōtōbees kan mitaakhuhr; we'll be back late Hanerga* mitaakhuhr; it's getting late el wa't etakhuhr; is it that late! dee saHeeH wakhree?; it's too late now el wa't mitaakhuhr delwa'tee; I'm a late riser ana dıman uhsHa mitakhur
lately min moda; I haven't seen him lately ana mashuftoosh min moda
later ba*dayn; later on ba*dayn; I'll come back later ana Harga* tanee; see you later ashoofak; no later than Tuesday lezim abl yum e-talaat
latest: the latest news akher akhbar; at the latest mush ba*d
laugh daHek; don't laugh matetHaksh; it's no laughing matter dee Haga madaHaksh
launderette, laundromat maghsalla afrangee
laundry (clothes) gheseel; (place) maghsalla; could you get the laundry done? mumkin teghsil el hidoom?
lavatory tawalet

law kaanoon; **against the law** duhd el kaanoon
lawn ard Hasheesh (f)
lawyer moHāmee
laxative mullayin
laze around: I just want to laze around mush *a-ɪyiz a*mil Haga
lazy kaslān; **don't be lazy** mateba'sh kaslān; **a nice lazy holiday** agezza hadee-a
lead (electrical) silk kaharaba; **where does this road lead?** e-taree' da yoo-wedee fayn?
leaf wara'
leaflet matboo-a*; **do you have any leaflets on ...?** fee matboo*aat *ala ...?
leak rashaH; **the roof leaks** esa'af beeyershaH
learn daras; **I want to learn ...** ana *a-ɪyiz adris ...
learner: I'm just a learner ana lessa mobtadi'
lease (verb) uhguhr
least: not in the least etlaakuhn; **at least 50** khamseen *alel a'al
leather gild
leave: when does the bus leave? el ōtōbees beeyetla* emta?; **I leave tomorrow** ana mashee bukra; **he left this morning** hoowa mishee e-subH; **may I leave this here?** mumkin esseeb da hena?; **I left my bag in the bar** ana sebt shantitee fil bar; **she left her bag here** haya sebit shantit-ha hena; **leave the window open please** seeb e-shebek maftooH lowsamaHt; **there's not much left** mafeesh keteer; **I've hardly any money left** ma*yeesh feloos keteer; **I'll leave it up to you** inta tekarar
Lebanese (man, adjective) libnānee; (woman) libnanaya
Lebanon libnan
lecherous shahwēnee
left shimēl; **on the left** *ala e-shimēl
left-hand drive drikseeyōn *ala e-shimēl

left-handed ashwel
left luggage office maktab amanēt
leg rigl (f)
legal shar*ɪ
lemon lamoon
lemonade espatis (tm)
lemon tea shay bi lamoon
lend selif; **would you lend me your ...?** mumkin tessalifnee ...?
lens (of camera) *adessa; **contact lenses** *adessēt laska; **I've lost one of my contact lenses** el *adessa da*ɪt minee
lens cap ghata *adessa
Lent e-soom el kebeer
less a'al; **less than an hour** a'al min sa*a; **less than that** a'al min kedda; **less expensive** arkhuhs
lesson dars; **do you give lessons?** inta biteddee diroos?
let: would you let me use it? mumkin tekhaleenee asta*milloo?; **will you let me know?** mumkin te*arafnee?; **I'll let you know** Hab' a'ōlak; **let me try** khaleenee aHawil; **let me go!** sibnamshee!; **let's leave now** yalla nimshee; **let's not go yet** khaleena shwɪya; **will you let me off at ...?** mumkin tenazilnee *and ...?; **apartments to let** sha'a mafroosha lil eegar
letter (in mail) gawab; (of alphabet) Harf; **are there any letters for me?** fee ay gawabaat laya?
letterbox sandoo' el busta
lettuce khass
level crossing mazla'ān
lever (noun) *atala
liable (responsible) mas'ool
liberated: a liberated woman sit Horra
library maktaba
Libya libya
Libyan (man, adjective) leebee; (woman) leebaya
licence, license rokhsa
license plate (on car) nimrit el *arabaya
lid ghata

lie (*untruth*) kizb; **can he lie down for a while?** mumkin hoowa yor'ud shwIya lowsamaHt?; **I want to go and lie down** ana *a-Iyiz arIaH shwIya

lie-in: I'm going to have a lie-in tomorrow ana HarIaH fi sireer bukra

life *omr; **not on your life!** da low Hatta *ala *omruhk!; **that's life!** e-donya kedda!

lifebelt tō' nageh

lifeboat markib inkaaz

lifeguard Hāris e-shaat

life insurance ta'meen *alel HIa

life jacket sutrit inkaaz

lift (*in hotel etc*) asuhnsayar; **could you give me a lift?** mumkin toowasuhlnee bil *arabaya?; **do you want a lift?** *a-Iyiznee awasuhluhk?; **thanks for the lift** shukran; **a friend gave me a lift** saHibee wosuhlnee

light (*noun*) noor; (*not heavy*) khafeef; **the light was on** e-noor kan welya*; **do you have a light?** (*for cigarette*) ma*ak kabreet?; **a light meal** akla khafeefa; **light blue** azra' fateH

light bulb lamba

lighter (*cigarette*) wala*a

lighter/lightest (*in weight*) akhaf

lighthouse fanar

light meter mi'yes fatHet el *adessa

lightning ra*d

like: I'd like a ... ana *a-Iyiz ...; **I'd like to ...** ana *a-Iyiz ...; **would you like a ...?** inta *a-Iyiz ...?; **would you like to come too?** leek mazeg teegee?; **I'd like to** atmanna; **I like it** baHebboo; **I like you** ana baHebbak; **I don't like it** mabaHebboosh; **he doesn't like it** hoowa mabeHebboosh; **do you like ...?** inta bitHebb ...?; **I like swimming** ana baHebb e-sibaHa; **OK, if you like** OK low teHebb; **what's it like?** zay ay?; **do it like this** kedda; **one like that** waaHid zay da

lime cordial, lime juice *aseer lamoon

line (*on paper*) satr; (*telephone*) khat;

(*of people*) taboor; **would you give me a line?** (*telephone*) mumkin tedeenee khat?

linen (*for beds*) bIyaadaat

linguist *alim bil loghēt; **I'm no linguist** ana mush kwIyis fil loghēt

lining bitaana

lion assad

lip shifa

lip brush forshit rooSH

lip gloss 'gloss'

lip pencil alam shefayf

lip salve zebda kakow

lipstick alam rooSH

liqueur sharab mo'atuhr

liquor koHol

list lista

listen: I'd like to listen to ... ana *a-Iyiz astimma* lee ...; **listen!** esma*!

liter, litre litr; *see page 118*

litter (*rubbish*) zibella

little sooghIar; **just a little, thanks** shwIya sooghIyara; **just a very little** shwIya sooghIyara awee; **a little cream** kreem mush keteer; **a little more** shwIya kamēn; **a little better** aHsen shwIya; **that's too little** (*not enough*) da mush kifaya

live sekin; **I live in ...** ana sekin fee ...; **where do you live?** inta sekin fayn?; **where does he live?** hoowa sekin fayn?; **we live together** eHna sekneen ma*aba*d

lively (*person, town*) nasheet

liver (*in body*) kibd; (*food*) kibda

lizard seHlaya

loaf *I-esh

lobby (*of hotel*) madkhal

lobster gambaree kebeer

local: local restaurant mat*am baladee; **local cheese** gibna baladee

lock (*noun*) ifl; **it's locked** ma'fool; **I locked myself out of my room** a' el bab et'afel wanna barra

locker (*for luggage etc*) amanēt

log I slept like a log ana nimt zay el mIyit

lollipop muhsaasa; (*ice lolly*) lollee-uhb

London 'london'

lonely waaнeed; **are you lonely?** inta waaнeed?

long taweel; **how long does it take?** bitekhud ad ay?; **is it a long way?** hoowa ba*yeed awee; **a long time** wa't tooweel; **I won't be long** mush нatakhuhr; **don't be long** matitakharsh; **that was long ago** da kan zamān; **I'd like to stay longer** ana *a-ıyiz a*d aktuhr; **long time no see!** mashooftaksh min zamān!; **so long!** ma*asalemma!

long distance call mokalmuh kharigaya

longer/longest atwuhl

loo: where's the loo? fayn el tawalet?; **I want to go to the loo** ana *a-ıyiz arooн li tawalet

look: that looks good da shaklō нelw; **you look tired** shaklak ta*ban; **I'm just looking, thanks** ana batfarag bas shukran; **you don't look your age** (*to a man*) inta shaklak sooghıyar; (*to a woman*) intee shaklik sooghıyar; **look at him** busilloo!; **I'm looking for ...** ana badowar *ala ...; **look out!** нasib!; **can I have a look?** mumkin abus?; **can I have a look around?** mumkin etfarag?

loose (*button, handle etc*) sayib

loose change fakka

lorry looree

lorry driver sawē' looree

lose khesir; **I've lost my ...** ana dıa*t ...; **I'm lost** ana tay-yeh

lost property office, lost and found maktab amanēt

lot: a lot, lots keteer; **not a lot** mush keteer; **a lot of money** feloos keteera; **a lot of women** sittet keteer; **a lot cooler** mitaaree; **I like it a lot** baнebboo keteer; **is it a lot further?** hoowa ba*yeed awee?; **I'll take the (whole) lot** нakhud-hum kuloohum

lotion lōshan

loud *alee; **the music is rather loud** el mooseeka *alee-a awee

lounge (*in house, hotel*) saala

lousy (*meal, hotel, holiday, weather*) mush kwıyis

love: I love you (*to a man*) baнebbak; (*to a woman*) baнebbik; **he's fallen in love** hoowa beeнebb; **I love Egypt** ana baнebb masr

lovely (*meal, view, weather, present etc*) gameel

low (*prices*) rekhees; (*bridge*) waatee

low beam e-noor el *adee

lower/lowest (*prices*) arkhus

LP istoo-waana

luck нuz; **hard luck!** 'hard luck'!; **good luck!** нuz sa*yeed!; **just my luck!** da bakhtee!; **it was pure luck** da kan нuz

lucky: that's lucky! da нuz!

lucky charm нegab

luggage shōnuht

lumbago 'lumbago'

lump (*medical*) waram

lunch gheda

lungs ri'atayn

luxurious (*hotel, furnishings*) moreeн giddan

luxury *ız

M

mad magnoon
madam madam
magazine migalla
magnificent (*view, day, meal*) momtaz
maid khadamit el ghoruhf
mail (*noun*) bareed; **is there any mail for me?** fee bareed laya?; **where can I mail this?** fayn sandoo' el busta?
mailbox sandoo' el busta
main ra'eesee; **where's the main post office?** fayn maktab el busta e-ra'eesee?
main road (*in town, in country*) e-taree' e-ra'eesee
maize dora
make *amil; **do you make them yourself?** bite*amilhum bee nafsak?; **it's very well made** da ma*mool kwIyis awee; **what does that make altogether?** kuloo bikam?; **I make it only 5 pounds** ana Hassabtoohum khamsa ginay
make-up mikyaaSH
make-up remover moozeel lil mikyaaSH
malaria malaree-a
male chauvinist pig anzooH
man raagil
manager mōdeer; **may I see the manager?** mumkin ashoof el mōdeer?
mango manga
manicure monōkeer
many keteer
map: **a map of ...** khareetit ...; **it's not on this map** mush fil khareeta dee
marble (*noun*) rōkhēm
March mēris
marijuana Hasheesh
mark: **there's a mark on it** *alee

*alēma; **could you mark it on the map for me?** mumkin te*alimoo *alel khareeta?
market (*noun*) soo'
marmalade 'marmalade'
married: **are you married?** (*to man*) inta mitgowz?; (*to woman*) intee mitgawizza?; **I'm married** ana mitgowz/mitgawizza
mascara 'mascara'
mast saaree
masterpiece toHfa
matches kabreet
material (*cloth*) omāsh; **what is this material?** el omāsh da ay?
matter: **it doesn't matter** ma*alesh; **what's the matter?** fee ay?
mattress martabba
Mauritania moritanya
Mauritanian (*man, adjective*) moritānee; (*woman*) moritanaya
maximum (*noun*) a*la Had
May mayoo
may: **may I have another coffee please?** mumkin ahwa tania lowsamaHt?; **may I?** mumkin?
maybe yimkin; **maybe not** yimkin la'
mayonnaise 'mayonnaise'
me: **come with me** ta*ala ma*ya; **it's for me** da *alashēnee; **it's me** ana; **me too** wana kamēn; *see page 106*
meal: **that was an excellent meal** el akla kanit momtaza; **does that include meals?** el akl maHsoob?
mean: **what does this word mean?** e-kelma dee ma*nēha ay?; **what does he mean?** hoowa uhzdoo ay?
measles el Hazba; **German measles** el Hazba el almanaya
measurements ma'assēt
meat laHma

Mecca makkuh; **towards Mecca** tigah makkuh

mechanic: do you have a mechanic here? fee mikaneekee hena?; **do you know where I can find a good mechanic?** inta te*ruhf mekaneekee kwɪyis?

medicine dowa (m)

medieval fil oroon el wusta

Mediterranean el baнr el mōtawassit

medium (adjective) mōtawassit

medium-sized mōtawassit

meet: pleased to meet you tasharuhfna; **where shall we meet?** nit'ābil fayn?; **let's meet up again** khaleena nit'ābil tanee

meeting egtima*

meeting place makkān egtima*

melon shamēma

member *odw; **I'd like to become a member** *a-ɪyiz ab'a *odw

mend: can you mend this? mumkin tisalaн da?

men's room tawalet

mention: don't mention it el *afw

menu kɪma; **may I have the menu please?** mumkin el kɪma lowsamaнt?

merchant tāgir

mess: it's a mess dee hargalla

message: are there any messages for me? fee akhbar *alashenee?; **I'd like to leave a message for ...** *a-ɪyiz aseeb khabar lil ...

metal (noun) ma*adan

metre, meter mitr; see page 117

midday: at midday e-dohr

middle: in the middle fi nus; **in the middle of the road** fi nus e-taree'

midnight: at midnight fi nus el layl

might: I might want to stay another 3 days ana gayz a*ad talat teeyem; **you might have warned me!** kunt *aruhftinee!

migraine suda* shedeed

mild (taste) mush нāmee; (weather) lateef

mile meel; **that's miles away!** da ba*yeed awee!; see page 117

military (adjective) нarbee

milk laban

millimetre, millimeter 'millimetre'

minaret ma'zanna

minced meat laнma mafrooma

mind: I don't mind ma*andeesh mane*a; **would you mind if I ...?** *andak mane*a low ana ...?; **never mind** ma*alesh; **I've changed my mind** ghɪyart ra'ee

mine: it's mine da bita*ee; see page 108

mineral water mɪya ma*adanaya

minimum (adjective) a'al

mint (sweet) ne*ana*

minus naa'is; **minus 3 degrees** talat daragaat taнt e-sifr

minute di'ee'a; **in a minute** kamen shwɪya; **just a minute** estanna shwɪya

mirror miraya

Miss anissa

miss: I miss you bitooнashnee; **there's a ... missing** fee ... naa'is; **we missed the bus** el ōtōbees fatna

mist shaboora

mistake ghalta; **I think there's a mistake here** azon fee ghalta hena

misunderstanding soo' tafēhum

mixture khaaleet

mix-up: there's been some sort of mix-up with ... kan fee soo' tafēhum ma*a ...

modern нadees

modern art fan нadees

moisturizer 'cream'

moment: I won't be a moment mush нatakhuhr

monastery dēr

Monday yum el itneen

money feloos (f); **I don't have any money** ma*eesh feloos; **do you take English/American money?** bitekhud istuhrleenee/dollaraat?

month shahr

monument tizkaar

moon uhмuhr

moorings marsa

moped biskilitta

more tanee; **may I have some more?** mumkin tanee?; **more coffee, please** ahwa tania lowsamaHt; **no more, thanks** da kifaya shukran; **more expensive** aghla; **more than 50** aktar min khamseen; **more than that** aktar min kedda; **a lot more** aktar; **I don't stay there any more** ana mush sēkkin hinak

morning subH; **good morning** sabaH el kheer; **this morning** e-naharda e-subH; **in the morning** e-subH

Morocco el maghrib

Moroccan maghribee

moslem muslim

mosque gāmi*a

mosquito namoosa

mosquito net shabakit namoos

most: I like this one most ana bafuhduhl da; **most of the time** mo*zuhm el wa't; **most hotels** mo*zuhm el fanādi'

mother um; **my mother** ummee

mother of pearl saduhf

motif (in pattern) zaghraffa

motor mator

motorbike mōtōsikl

motorboat luhnsh

motorist sawē'

motor yacht yakht

mountain gabbal; **up in the mountains** fil gabbal; **a mountain village** kaaria fil gabbal

mouse far

moustache shanab

mouth bo'

move: he's moved to another hotel hoowa na'al li fondō' tanee; **could you move your car?** mumkin tin'il *arabeeyetuhk?

movie film; **let's go to the movies** yalla nerooH e-sinima

movie camera kamira sinima-aya

movie theater 'cinema'

moving: a very moving tune naghama tera'as

Mr ōstez

Mrs madam

Ms no equivalent

much keteer; **much better** aHsen keteer; **much cooler** abruhd; **not much** mush keteer; **not so much** mush keteer

muezzin mo'azin

muffler (car) *albit e-shakmān

mug: I've been mugged ana etsar'at

muggy: it's very muggy e-rotooba *alia awee

mule gaHsh

mummy (in tomb) momee-a

mumps eltihab fil gōdad

murals (paintings) risoom milawina; (hieroglyphics) ni'oosh milawina

muscle *adala

museum matHaf

music museeka; **kanoon music** museekat anoon; **do you have the sheet music for ...?** *andak e-nōta el musikaya lil ...?

musician musikaar

mussels om el khilool

must: I must ... ana lezim ...; **I mustn't drink ...** ana mamnoo-a* min shorb ...; **you mustn't forget** matinsesh

mustache shanab

my: my room ōtee; **my ticket** tazkatee; see page 105

myself: I'll do it myself Ha*amiloo bi nafsee

N

nail (*of finger*) dofr; (*in wood*) musmar
nail clippers asaafit dowaafir
nailfile mabruhd dowaafir
nail polish milamma* lil dowaafir
nail polish remover tenir
nail scissors ma'as dowaafir
naked *ɪree-ēn
name ism; what's your name? ismak
ay?; what's its name? ismhoo ay?;
my name is ... ismee ...
nap: he's having a nap hoowa
biyēkhud ghefwit num
napkin (*serviette*) foota
nappy kafoola
nappy-liners *azl nabee
narrow (*road*) day-yeh'
nasty (*taste, person, weather, cut*) fazee-
a*
national dowlee
nationality ginsaya
natural tabee*ɪyee
naturally (*of course*) tab*an; (*in a
natural way*) bi taba*
nature (*trees etc*) tabee*a
nausea bi suda*
nauseous: I'm feeling nauseous ana
Hassis bi suda*
near gamb; is it near here? hoowa
orɪyib min hena?; near the window
gamb e-shebek; do you go near ...?
inta bit*adee *ala ...?; where is the
nearest ...? fayn a'rab ...?
nearby orɪyib awee
nearly ta'reeban
nearside wheel el *agala el orɪyibba
neat (*room etc*) uhneek; (*drink*) lee
waHdo
necessary darooree; is it necessary
to ...? hoowa darooree lee ...?; it's
not necessary mush darooree
neck (*of body*) ra'ba; (*of dress, shirt*)

ye'ah
necklace *a'od
necktie garafatta
need: I need a ... ana meHtag ...; do
I need a ...? aHtag ...?; it needs
more salt meHtag shwɪyit malHa;
there's no need maloosh lezoom;
there's no need to shout! maloosh
lezoom teeza*a'!
needle ibra
negative (*film*) *afreet
neighbo(u)r gar
neighbo(u)rhood geera
neither: neither of us wala waaHid
minna; neither one (of them) wala
waaHid fee hum; neither ... nor ...
la ... wala ...; neither do I walana;
neither does he wala hoowa
nephew (*brother's son*) ibn akh; (*sister's
son*) ibn okht
nervous *asabee
net (*fishing, tennis*) shabakuh
neurotic ekhteelal el a*saab
neutral (*gear*) filmoor
never abadan
new gedeed; new moon hilāl
news akhbar (*f*); is there any news?
fee ay akhbar?
newspaper gurnaan; do you have
any English newspapers? *andak ay
gurɪyid ingileezee?
newsstand bɪya* gurɪyid
New Year e-sana e-gedeeda; Happy
New Year *a-am gedeed sa*yeed
New Year's Eve laylit raas e-sana
New York 'new york'
New Zealand nyoozlanda
New Zealander (*man*) nyoozlandee;
(*woman*) nyoozlandaya
next: the next one ellee ba*dō; it's at
the next corner *and e-nassia ellee

gaya; **next week** el isbooa* e-gay;
next Monday litneen e-gay; **next to
the post office** gamb el busta; **the
one next to that** el waaHid ellee
gamb da
nextdoor (*adverb, adjective*) el bayt
ellee gambenna
next of kin areeb
nice (*person, meal, town, day*) kwIyis;
that's very nice of you da zo'
minak; **a nice cold drink** mashroob
se'a* awee
nicer/nicest aHla
nickname ism e-dalla*
niece (*brother's daughter*) bint akh;
(*sister's daughter*) bint okht
night layl; **for one night** lee mōdit
layla waHda; **for three nights** lee
mōdit talaat layalee; **good night**
tisbaH *ala kheer; **at night** bil layl
nightclub malha laylee (*m*)
nightdress amees num
night flight reHla laylayla
nightie amees num
night-life HIyat e-layl
nightmare kaboos
night porter ghefeer
Nile nahr e-neel
nits (*bugs, in hair*) aml
no la'; **I've no money** ma*I-eesh
feloos; **there's no more** mafeesh; **no
more than ...** mush aktar min ...; **oh
no!** (*upset*) akh!
nobody mafeesh Had, wala waaHid
noise dowsha
noisy *amil dowsha; **it's too noisy** da
dowsha awee
nomad badawee
non-alcoholic min gheer koHol;
non-alcoholic drink mashroobaat
gheer kaHolaya
none wala Haga, mafeesh; **none of
them** wala waaHid fee hum
nonsense kalēm fērigh

non-smoking (*compartment, section of
plane*) mamnoo*a e-tadkheen
non-stop (*travel*) *alatool
no-one mafeesh Had, wala waaHid
nor: nor do I walana; **nor does he**
wala hoowa
normal *adee
north shimēl; **to the north** li shimēl
northeast e-shimēl e-shar'ee; **to the
northeast** li shimēl e-shar'ee
Northern Ireland irlanda e-
shamalaya
northwest e-shimēl el ghaarbee; **to
the northwest** li shimēl el ghaarbee
Norway norweeg
nose marakheen; **my nose is bleeding**
marakheenee bitgeeb dam
not mush; **I don't smoke**
mabadakhansh; **he didn't say anything** hoowa ma'elsh aya Haga; **it's
not important** mush mōhim; **not
that one** mush da; **not for me** mush
*alashēnee; *see page 112*
note (*bank note*) wara'; (*written message
etc*) moozakerra
notebook nōta
nothing mafeesh Haga, wala Haga
November novimbuhr
now delwa'tee; **not now** mush
delwa'tee
nowhere wala Hetta
nuisance: he's being a nuisance
(*pestering woman etc*) hoowa mida-
y'inee
numb (*limb etc*) minamil
number (*figure*) nimra; **what number?**
nimra kam?
number plates nimer el *arabaya
nurse momaredduh
nursery (*at airport etc, for children*)
Hadaana
nut gōz; (*for bolt*) samoola
nutter: he's a nutter (*is crazy*) hoowa
magnoon

O

oar migdaf

oasis waHa; at the oasis fil waHa

obelisk misella

obligatory igbāree

oblige: much obliged (thank you) shukran

obnoxious (person) fazee-a*

obstetrician akhissaa'ee uhmraad el wilāda

obvious: that's obvious da waadeH

occasionally aHeeyēnan

o'clock e-sa*a; see page 116

October oktōbuhr

octopus akhtaboot

odd (strange) ghereeb; (number) fardee

odometer *adad el masafēt

of: the name of the hotel ism el fondō'; the owner of the car saaHeb el *arabaya; the price of the tickets taman e-tazkara; have one of mine khud waaHid min bita*ee; see page 108

off: 20% off takhfeed *ashreen fil maya; the lights were off e-noor kan matfee; just off the main road taHweeda waHda min e-tahree' el *amoomee

offend: don't be offended matiz*alsh

office (place of work) maktab

officer (said to policeman) effendim

official (noun) mas'ool; is that official? da rasmee?

off-season mush fil moosim

off-side wheel el *agala el bay*yeeda

often dIman; not often aHyennan

oil (for car, for salad) zayt; (crude oil) bitrōl; it's losing oil bitsarab zayt; will you change the oil? mumkin teghIyar e-zayt?; the oil light's flashing kashef e-zayt baynowar

oil fields Hokool el bitrōl

oil painting rasma alwān bi zayt

oil pressure daght e-zayt

oil rigs ag-hizza listikhraag el bitrōl

oil tanker (ship) na'lit bitrōl

oil well aabaar bitrōl

ointment marhuhm

OK 'ok'; are you OK? inta kwIyis?; that's OK thanks da tamem, shukran; that's OK by me ana mowafi'

old (thing) adeem; (person) *agooz; how old are you? *andak kam sana?

old age pensioner kebeer fi sin

old-fashioned mōda adeema

old town (old part of town) ... el adeema; Old Cairo masr el'adeema

olive zetoon

olive oil zayt zetoon

Oman *amān

Omani (man, adjective) *amānee; (woman) *amanaya

omelet(t)e omlit

on *ala; on the roof *ala suht-H; on the beach *alel bilasH; on Friday yum el gom*a; on television fi teleevizyōn; I don't have it on me mush ma*aya; this drink's on me el mashroob da *alaya; a book on Cairo kitab *an el kaheera; the warning light comes on noor e-teeHzeer beenawar; the light was on e-noor kan wēle*a; what's on in town? fee ay fil balad?; it's just not on! (not acceptable) da mayinfa*sh

once (one time) mara waHda; at once (immediately) delwa'tee

one waaHid; (for feminine nouns) waHda; that one da; the green one el waaHid el akhdar; the one with the black skirt on el waHda ellee labsa goonilla sōdaa; **the one in the blue shirt** el waaHid ellee labis amees azra'

onion basal

only bas; **only one** waaHid bas; **only once** mara waHda bas; **it's only 9 o'clock** e-sa*a tissa* bas; **I've only just arrived** ana lessa waasil

open (*adjective*) fateH; **when do you open?** biteftaH emta?; **in the open** (*in open air*) fil khala; **it won't open** mush *a-Iyiz yitfeteH

opening times mowa*Id el *amel

open top (*car*) makshoof

opera obra

operation (*medical*) *amilaya

operator (*telephone*) *amil e-telefōnet, e-switsh

opportunity forsa

opposite: opposite the mosque ōdam e-gāmi*a; **it's directly opposite** ōdam bizobt

oppressive (*heat*) (*colloquial word*) shedeeda; (*formal word*) sa*ab el eHtimel

optician akhisaa'ee nuhdaaraat

optimistic mutafe'il

optional ekhtee-yeree

or ow

orange (*fruit*) bortoo'an; (*colour*) bortoo'aanee

orange juice (*fresh*) *aseer bortoo'an taaza; (*fizzy, diluted*) *aseer bortoo'an

orchestra 'orchestra'

order: could we order now? (*in restaurant*) mumkin nutlub delwa'tee?; **I've already ordered** ana talubt khaalas; **I didn't order that** ana matalubtish da; **it's out of order** (*lift etc*) mush shaghēl

ordinary *adee

organization (*company*) shirka

organize nuhzuhm; **could you organize it?** mumkin tenuhzuhmoo?

original aslee; **is it an original?** da aslee?

ornament zeena

ostentatious (*clothes, colour etc*) mifakhfakh

other tanee; **the other waiter** el garsōn e-tanee; **the other one** el waahid e-tanee; **are there any others?** fee tanee?; **some other time, thanks** wa'at tanee, shukran

otherwise wa illa

ouch! Iyee!

ought: he ought to be here soon hoowa mafrood yeekoon hena ba*d shwIya

ounce *see page 118*

our: our home baytna; **our suitcases** shōnuhtna; **to our hotel** lil fondō; *see page 105*

ours bita*anna; **that's ours** da bita*anna; *see page 108*

out: he's out hoowa bara; **get out!** okhrug bara!; **I'm out of money** ma*I-eesh feloos; **a few kilometres out of town** bara el balad shwIya

outboard (motor) mator

outdoors bara

outlet (*electrical*) bareeza

outside bara; **can we sit outside?** mumkin no'a*od bara?

outskirts: on the outskirts of ... fee dawaHee ...

oven forn

over: over here hena; **over there** hinak; **over 100** fo' el maya; **I'm burnt all over** ana etHarra't min e-shams; **the holiday's over** el agēzza khalsit

overcharge: you've overcharged me inta khat feloos keteer

overcoat baltoo

overcooked mistiwee awee

overexposed (*photograph*) minnawarra

overheat: it's overheating (*car*) el mator beeyeskhan

overland (*travel*) bi taree'

overlook: overlooking the sea yootul *ala el baHr

overnight (*travel*) tool e-layl

oversleep: I overslept ana etakhart fi num

overtake *ada

overweight (*person*) fo' el wazn

owe: how much do I owe you? ana

*alaya kam?

own: my own ... ...-ee; my own house baytee; **my own daughter** bintee; **my own money** feloosee; **are you on your own?** inta lee

waHdak?; **I'm on my own** ana lee waHdee

owner (*colloquial word*) saaHib; (*more formal word*) mālik

oyster maHarr

P

pack: a pack of cigarettes *albit saggayar; **I'll go and pack** ana Harooн asta*id

package (*at post office*) tard

package holiday reнla shamla

package tour reнla shamla

packed out: the place was packed out el makkan kan zaнma awee

packet *albuh; **a packet of cigarettes** *albit saggayar

paddle (*noun*) migdaf

padlock (*noun*) ifl

page (*of book*) suhf-Huh; **could you page Mr ...?** mumkin tinādee el ōstez ...?

pain waga*; **I have a pain here** *andee waga* hena

painful mo'lim

painkillers musakin

paint (*oil paint*) lōn zayt; (*water colours*) alwān mīya; (*on car*) dihan; **I'm going to do some painting** (*artist*) ana rīaн arsim

paintbrush (*artist's*) forshit alwān

painting soora

pair: a pair of ... itneen min ...

pajamas bisнaama

Pakistan bakistan

Pakistani (*man, adjective*) bakistānee; (*woman*) bakistanaya

pal saaHib

palace asr

pale (*face*) misfuhr; (*colour*) fateн; **pale blue** azra' fateн

Palestine falasteen

Palestinian (*man,   adjective*)

falasteenee; (*woman*) falasteenaya

palm tree nakhla

palpitations nuhbd

pancake feteera

panic: don't panic matit-re*absh

panties kulot Hareemee

pants (*trousers*) bantalōn; (*underpants*) kulot

panty girdle korsay

pantyhose sharab filay

paper wara'; (*newspaper*) gurnaan; **a piece of paper** Hettit wara'

paper handkerchiefs manadeel wara'

papyrus wara' el baardee

paraffin barafeen

parallel: parallel to ... moo-wazee lee ...

parasol shamsaya Hareemee

parcel tard

parched (*land, person*) gaf

pardon (me)? (*didn't understand*) na*m?

parents: my parents waldee wee walditee

park (*noun*) mow'af; **where can I park?** arkin fayn?; **there's nowhere to park** mafeesh makkān arkin fee

parking lights e-noor el waatee

parking lot mō'af *arabeeyaat

parking place: there's a parking place! fee makkān terkin fee!

part (*noun*) guz'

partner (*boyfriend*) saHibee; (*girlfriend*) saHbitee; (*in business*) shireek

party (*group*) magmoo*a; (*celebration*) Hafla; **let's have a party** yalla ne*amil Hafla

pass (*in mountains*) momarr; (*verb: overtake*) saba'; **he passed out** oghma *alay; **he made a pass at me** hoowa Hawil ma*aya

passable (*road*) saaleH li sawē'a

passenger rēkib

passport bassbort

past: in the past fil maadee; **just past the bank** ba*d el bank; **half past two** itneen wi nus; *see page 116*

pastry (*dough*) *ageena; (*small cake*) feteera

patch: could you put a patch on this? mumkin tekhı-uht da?

path momarr

patient: be patient osborr

patio varanduh

pattern batrōn; **a dress pattern** batrōn; **I like the pattern on that ...** baHebb e-tuhsmeem ellee *alal ...

paunch kirsh

pavement (*sidewalk*) raseef

pay (*verb*) dafa*; **can I pay, please?** mumkin adfa* lowsamaHt?; **it's already paid for** el Hisab khaalis; **I'll pay for this** Hadfa* lee da

pay phone telefōn *amoomee

peace salam

peace and quiet heedoo'

peach khōkhaa

peanuts fool sudānee

pear komitra

pearl loolee

peas bisilla

peasant fellaH

peculiar (*taste, custom*) ghereeb

pedal (*in car*) dawāsa; (*on bike*) beedal

pedestrian mushēh

pedestrian crossing *aboor mushēh

pedestrian precinct lil mushēh faakuht

pedicure 'pedicure'

pee: I need to go for a pee lezim arooH li tawalet

peg (*for washing*) masHbak; (*for tent*) wattad

pen alam; **do you have a pen?** ma*ak alam?

pencil alam roosaas

penfriend saadee' morasla; **shall we be penfriends?** mumkin nitrēssil?

penicillin bensilleen

penknife matoowa

pen pal saadee' morasla

pensioner *agooz

people nās; **a lot of people** nās keteer; **the Egyptian people** el masrayeen

pepper (*spice*) filfil eswid; **green pepper** filfil akhdar; **red pepper** filfil aHmar

peppermint (*sweet*) nea*na*

per: per night fil layla; **how much per hour?** beekam e-sa*a?

per cent fil maya

perfect tamem

perfume reeHa

perhaps gayz

period (*of time*) mōda; (*menstruation*) el *aada

perm kanteesh

permit (*noun*) tuhsreeH

Persian Gulf el khaleeg el farisee

person shaakhs

pessimistic mutashē'im

petrol benzeen

petrol can suhfeeHet benzeen

petrol station maHattit benzeen

petrol tank (*in car*) 'tank'

petrol tanker (*truck*) *arabayit na'l benzeen

pharmacy agzakhēnna

Pharaoh far*ōn

phone *see* **telephone**

photogenic: she is very photogenic haya Helwa awee fi siwuhr

photograph (*noun*) soora; **would you take a photograph of us?** mumkin tessawurna?

photographer mussawaraatee

phrase: a useful phrase gomla mufeeda

phrasebook daleel seeyaHee

pianist *azif beeyanō

piano beeyanō

piastre uhrsh

pickpocket nashēl

pick up: when can I pick them up? (*clothes from laundry etc*) emta āgee akhudhum?; **will you come and pick me up?** mumkin teegee tekhudnee?

picnic (*noun*) nōzha

picture soora

piece Hetta; **a piece of ...** Hettit ...

pig khanzeer

pigeon Hamāma

piles (*medical*) el bawaseer

pile-up (*crash*) Hadsa

pilgrim Hag

pilgrimage Heg; **have you made a pilgrimage to Mecca yet?** inta Hagit?

pill Habba; **I'm on the pill** ana bēkhud Heboob manna* el Haml

pillar *amood

pillarbox sandoo' busta

pillow makhadda

pillow case kees makhadda

pin (*noun*) daboos

pineapple ananas

pineapple juice *aseer ananas

pink bamba

pint *see page 119*

pipe (*for smoking*) beeba; (*for water*) masoora

pipe cleaner monuhzif beeba

pipeline anabeeb bitrōl

pipe tobacco dokhēn beeba

pity: it's a pity ma*alesh

pizza beetza

place (*noun*) makkān; **is this place taken?** Had a*ıd hena?; **would you keep my place for me?** mumkin tekhelee bālak min makēnee?; **at my place** fee baytee; **at your place** fee baytak

plain (*food*) *adee; (*not patterned*) sēda

plane tıyara

plant nabat

plaster cast ālib gibs

plastic blastik

plastic bag shanta blastik

plate taba'

platform raseef; **which platform, please?** raseef nimra kam

lowsamaHt?

play (*verb*) le*ıb; (*noun: in theatre*) muhsraHaya

playboy blay boy

playground malla*b

pleasant sar

please lowsamaHt; **yes please** ıwa lowsamaHt; **could you please ...?** mumkin ... lowsamaHt?

plenty: plenty of ... keteer min ...; **that's plenty, thanks** da kifaya shukran

pleurisy eltihab el bilyora

pliers zaradaya

plonk (*wine*) nebeet; (*cheap wine*) nebeet rekhees

plug (*electrical*) feesha; (*for car*) tuhbit el kartēr; (*in sink*) suhdēdit Hōd

plughole *ın el Hōd

plum bar'oo'a

plumber sabēk

plus (*arithmetic*) zē'id

p.m. ba*d e-dohr; **at 2.00 p.m.** e-sa*a itneen ba*d e-dohr; **at 10.00 p.m.** e-sa*a *ashara bil layl

pneumonia eltihab e-re'a

pocket gib; **in my pocket** fee geebee

pocketbook (*woman's handbag*) shantit eed

pocketknife matwa

point: could you point to it? mumkin teshēwer *allay?; **four point six** arba* wi sitta min *ashara; **there's no point** mafeesh fıda

points (*in car*) ablateen

poison sim

poisonous musamim

police bolees; **call the police!** etessil bil bolees!

policeman *askaree; (*higher rank, with stars*) zaabit

police station esm e-shorta

polish (*noun*) warneesh; **will you polish my shoes?** mumkin telama* gazmitee?

polite mo'adab

politician seeyēsee

politics *a-elm e-seeyēssa

polluted millawis

pomegranate romaana
pond birka
pony see-see
pool (*for swimming*) Hammem sibaHa; (*game*) billeeyardō
poor (*not rich*) fē'eer; (*quality*) mush kwIyis; **poor old Mohamed!** ye*Inee *ala moHammad!
Pope el baabaa
pop music mooseeka gharbaya; (*western*) mooseeka afrangee
popsicle (*tm*) lollee-uhb
pop singer mōghānee
popular maHboob
population e-sha*ab
port (*for boats*) meena; (*drink*) bōrt
porter (*in hotel, at station*) shIyel
portrait soora
Portugal bortooghel
poser: he is a poser hoowa shayif nafsoo
posh (*restaurant*) fēkhir giddan; (*people*) fo'awee
possibility eHtimal
possible: is it possible to ...? mumkin ...?; **as ... as possible** bee ... mIyumkim
post (*noun: mail*) busta; **could you post this for me?** mumkin termee el gawab da fil busta?
postbox sandoo' busta
postcard kart
poster (*advertisement*) ē*alēn; (*as souvenir*) soora
poste restante *you have a post box number:* sandoo' bareed rakuhm
post office maktab bareed; (*colloquial word*) el busta
pot (*for cooking*) edra; (*teapot*) baraad shay; **a pot of tea for two** shay litneen
potato bataatis (*f*)
potato chips bataatis maHamarra
potato salad salaatit bataatis
pots and pans (*cooking implements*) Hellel
pottery (*objects*) khazaf; (*workshop*) masna* khazaf
pound (*Egyptian money*) ginay; (*British*)

estirleenee; *see page 118*
pour: it's pouring down bitnuhtuhr gāmid
powder (*for face*) budra
powdered milk laban budra
power cut el kaharaba ma'too*a; **there's been a power cut** el kaharaba etatIt
power point bareeza
power station maHattit towleed el kaharaba
practise, practice: I need to practise meHtag tamreen
pram *arabit tefl
prawn cocktail koktayl gambaree
prawns gambaree
prayer salaa
prefer: I prefer ... ana afuhduhl ...
preferably: preferably not tomorrow el aHsen mush bukra
pregnant Hāmil
prescription (*for chemist*) rooshetta
present (*gift*) hidaya; **here's a present for you** (*to a man*) hidaya *alashēnak; (*to a woman*) hidaya *alashēnik; **at present** delwa'tee
president (*of company, country*) ra'ees
press: could you press these? mumkin tekwee dōl?
pretty gameel; **it's pretty expensive** da ghēlee awee
price taman
prickly heat Hamooneel
priest assees
prime minister ra'ees el wozuh-ruh
prince ameer
princess ameera
print (*noun: picture*) soora
printed matter muhtbō*aat
priority (*in driving*): **it was my priority** da kan taree'ee
prison sig-n
private khaas; **private bath** bi Hammēm
prize gayza
probably gayz
problem mushkilla; **I have a problem** *andee mushkilla; **no problem!** mafeesh mushkilla!

program(me) (*noun*) birnāmig
promise: I promise aw*ıdak; **is that
a promise?** da wa*d?
**pronounce: how do you pronounce
this?** izzay tintuh' da?; **I can't
pronounce it** mush adir a'ooloo
properly kwıyis; **it's not repaired
properly** matsuhllaнsh kwıyis
prophet nabee
prostitute moomis
protect saan
protein remover (*for contact lenses*)
maнlool lituhndeef
Protestant brotistant
proud fakhoor
prunes bar'oo nashif
public (*adjective*) *amoomee
public convenience tawalet
public holiday agēzza rasmaya
pudding нelw
pull shad; **he pulled out without in-
dicating** hoowa tela* min gheer
mıyeddee eshara
pullover bullōvar

pump (*for water*) toolomba; (*for bike*)
minfēkh; (*for car*) howa
punctual: he is punctual hoowa
moнaafiz *ala el mo-a*ıd
puncture (*noun*) khorm
pure (*silk etc*) saafee
pure orange juice bortoo'aan khaalis
purple banafsigee
purse (*for money*) kees; (*handbag*)
shanta
push za'; **don't push in!** matzo'ish
push-chair *arabit tefl
put нott; **where did you put ...?** inta
нattit fayn ...?; **where can I put ...?**
aнott ... fayn?; **could you put the
lights on?** mumkin too-ala* e-noor?;
will you put the light out? mumkin
tetfee e-noor?; **you've put the price
up** inta *alayt e-sa*r; **could you put
us up for the night?** mumkin
naynām hena elleelādee?
pyjamas bisнaama
pyramid haram; **the Pyramids** el
ahramaat

Q

Qatar kuhtuhr
Qatari min kuhtuhr
quality nōwa; **poor quality** nōwa*
mush kwıyis; **good quality** nōwa
kwıyis
quarantine нaguhr seнee
quart *see page 119*
quarter rub'a*; **quarter of an hour**
rub'a* sa*a; *see page 116*
quay marsa
quayside: on the quayside нafit el
marsa
queen malika; (*cards*) bint
question soo'el; **that's out of the**

question da mush mumkin
queue (*noun*) taboor; **there was a big
queue** kan fee taboor taweel
quick saree*; **that was quick** da
saree* awee; **which is the
quickest way?** ay asra* taree'?
quicker/quickest asra*
quickly bisor*a
quiet (*place, hotel*) haddee; **be quiet!**
hidoo' lowsamaнt!
quinine kineen
quite: quite a lot keteer awee; **it's quite
different** da mokhtalif awee; **I'm not
quite sure** ana mush mōta-akid

R

rabbit arnab

rabies da' el kalb

race (*noun: for horses, cars etc*) seebe';
I'll race you there ana Hazba'k
hinak

racket (*sport*) muhdruhb

radiator (*of car, in room*) raydater

radio radyō; **on the radio** *ala radyō

rag (*for cleaning*) kohna

rail: by rail bi sikka el Hadeed

railroad, railway e-sikka el Hadeed

railroad crossing mazla'an

rain (*noun*) nuhtara; **in the rain** fi
nuhtara; **it's raining** bitnuhtuhr

rape (*noun*) eghteesaab

rare (*object etc*) nadir; (*steak*) mush
mistiwee awee

rash (*on skin*) tuhfH

rat far

rate (*for changing money*) se*ar; **what's
the rate for the pound?** ay se*ar el
estuhrleenee?; **what are your rates?**
(*at car hire etc*) as*aruhk ay?

rather: it's rather late dee wakhree
shwIya; **I'd rather ...** ana afuhduhl
...; **I'd rather have rice** ana
afuhduhl ruz

raw (*meat*) nay

razor (*dry, electric*) makanit Hila'a

razor blades amwes Hila'a

reach: within easy reach orIyib

read kara'; **I can't read it** mush a'dar
a'ra; **could you read it out?** mumkin
tea'ra bisōt *alee?; **I want to learn to
read Arabic** ana *a-Iyiz at*allim
*arabee

ready gehiz; **when will it be ready?**
HIkoon gehiz emta?; **I'll go and get
ready** ana rIaH asta*id; **I'm not
ready yet** ana mush gehiz

real Ha'ee-ee

really awee; **I really must go** ana
lezim amshee; **is it really necessary?**
da darooree awee?

realtor maktab simsar

rear: at the rear fil akhir

rear wheels el *agal el waraanee

rearview mirror mirraya

reasonable (*prices etc*) ma*'ool; **be
reasonable** khaleek ma*'ool

receipt wasl

recently min orIyib

reception (*in hotel*) isti'bel; (*for guests*)
Haflit isti'bel

reception desk el isti'bel

receptionist moowazuhf isti'bel

recipe wasfa; **can you give me the
recipe for this?** mumkin tedeenee el
wasfa?

recognize et*aruhf *al; **I didn't
recognize it** ma*reftoohoosh

**recommend: could you recommend
...?** mumkin te'olee ...?

record (*noun: music*) istoowaana

record player bikuhb

red aHmar

Red Sea el baHr el aHmar

red wine nebeet aHmar

reduction (*in price*) takhfeed

reeds gheb

refinery ma*mal takreer bitrōl

refreshing mon*ash

refrigerator talaga

refund targee*; **do I get a refund?**
mumkin araga* da?; **no refund**
mafeesh targee*a

region monte'a

registered: by registereed mail
bareed musagil

registration number nimrit el
*arabaya

relative: my relatives areebee

relaxing: it's very relaxing da mohadee awee

reliable (*person, car*) ameen

religion deen

religious (*person*) mōtadayin

remains (*of old city etc*) kharabaat

remember: I don't remember mush fakir; **I remember** ana fakir; **do you remember?** inta fakir?

remote (*village etc*) ba*yeed

rent (*noun: for apartment etc*) igar; (*verb: car etc*) uhguhr; **I'd like to rent a bike/car** ana a*ıyiz a-uhguhr *agala/*arabaya

rental car *arabaya mituhgara

repair (*verb*) suhllaH; **can you repair it?** mumkin tisalaH da?

repeat karrar; **could you repeat that?** mumkin tekarrar tanee?

representative (*noun: of company*) ne'ib

request (*noun*) tuhluhb

rescue (*verb*) uhnkuhz

reservation Hagz; **I have a reservation** *ana Hagazt hena

reserve Hagaz; **I reserved a room in the name of ...** ana Hagazt ōda bee ism ...; **can I reserve a table for tonight?** mumkin aHgiz tarabayza lil layla dee?

rest (*repose*) raHa; (*remainder*) be'ee; **I need a rest** meHtag istiraHa; **the rest of the group** be'ee el magmoo*a

restaurant mat*am

rest house istiraHa

rest room tawalet

retired: I'm retired ana *alel ma*ash

return: a return to Cairo tazkarit *a-ooda lil kaheera; **I'll return it tomorrow** ana Haraga*ha bukra

returnable: is this returnable? da kaabil lil targee*?

reverse gear marshidayar

revolting mo'rif

rheumatism 'rheumatism'

rib dilla*; **a cracked rib** dilla* maksoor

ribbon (*for hair*) shireet

rice ruz

rich (*person*) ghenee; (*food*) dism; **it's too rich** dism awee

ride: can you give me a ride into town? mumkin te-wasuhlnee lee nus el balad?; **thanks for the ride** shukran

ridiculous: that's ridiculous da ginoon

right (*correct*) saH; (*not left*) yimeen; **you're right** inta *ala Ha'; **you were right** inta kunt *ala Ha'; **that's right** da saH; **that can't be right** da mush saH; **right!** saH!; **is this the right road for ...?** da e-taree' lil ...?; **on the right** *alel yimeen; **turn right** Howid yimeen; **not right now** mush delwa'tee

right-hand drive direkseeyōn *alel yimeen

ring (*in finger*) khetim; **I'll ring you** Haatissil beek

ring road taree' da'ēree

ripe (*fruit*) mistiwee

rip-off: it's a rip-off dee ser'a; **rip-off prices** as*ar khayalaya

risky khuhtuhr; **it's too risky** khuhtuhr awee

river nahr; **by the river** gamb e-nahr

road taree'; **is this the road to ...?** da taree' lil ...?; **further down the road** ōdam shwıya

road accident Hadsa

road hog sawe' magnoon

road map khareetit toro'

roadside: by the roadside *ala gamb e-taree'

roadsign esharit toro'

roadwork(s) tuhsleeH toro'

roast beef rōz beef

rob: I've been robbed anatsara't

robe (*housecoat*) rōb shambuhr

rock (*stone*) Hagguhr; **on the rocks** (*with ice*) bee talg

rocky (*coast etc*) sakhree

roll (*bread*) feeno medowar

Roman rōmānee; **Roman ruins** asaar rōmanaya

Roman Catholic kathōleekee

romance kesit Hobb
roof suht-H; **on the roof** *alel suht-H;
  can we sleep on the roof? mumkin
  ninam fi suH-t?
roof rack shabakit *arabaya
room ōda; **do you have a room?**
  *andak ōda?; **a room for two people**
  ōda litneen; **a room for three nights**
  ōda lee talateeyem; **a room with a**
  bathroom ōda bi Hammem; **in my**
  room fee ōtee; **there's no room**
  mafeesh maken
room service khedma lil aywad
rope Habl
rose warda
rosé (*wine*) wardee
Rosetta stone Haggar rasheed
rough (*sea*) hayig; (*crossing*) sa*ab; **the**
  engine sounds a bit rough fee *Iyib
  fil mator; **I've been sleeping rough**
  (*in open air*) ana nimt fil khala
roughly (*approximately*) ta'reeban
roulette 'roulette'
round (*adjective*) medowar; **it's my**
  round da dooree
round-trip: a round-trip ticket to ...

tazkarit *a-ooda lil ...
route taree'; **what's the best route?** ay
  aHsen taree'?
rowboat, rowing boat markib
rubber (*material*) mataat; (*eraser*)
  asteeka
rubber band astik
rubbish (*waste*) zibella; (*poor quality*
  goods) nōwa* mush kwIyis; **that's**
  rubbish! (*nonsense*) da kalem faadee
rucksack shanta li dahr
rude mush mo'adab; **he was very**
  rude hoowa kan aleel el adab
rug sigada
ruins kharabaat
rum 'rum'; **rum and coke** 'rum' wa
  kakōla
run (*person*) geree; **I go running**
  (*habitually*) ana bagree; **quick, run!**
  egree bisor*a!; **how often do the**
  buses run? el ōtōbees beeyetla* kul
  ad ay?; **he's been run over** hoowa
  indes; **I've run out of gas/petrol**
  mafeesh benzeen
rupture (*medical*) fat'
Russia russya

S

saccharine sookaree
sad Hazeen
saddle (*for bike*) korsee; (*for horse*) sirg
safe (*not in danger*) kwIyis; (*not danger-*
  ous) amān; **will it be safe here?**
  Hatkoon amān hena?; **is it safe to**
  drink? dee salHa li shorb?; **is it a**
  safe beach for swimming? da bilasH
  amān li sibaHa?; **could you put this**
  in your safe? mumkin tisheel da fee
  khaznetak?
safety pin daboos masHbak
Sahara saHara
sail (*noun*) shiraa*; **let's go sailing**
  yalla nerooH 'sailing'

sailboard (*noun*) 'sailboard'
sailboarding: I like sailboarding ana
  baHebb 'windsurfing'
sailor baHarr
salad salaata
salad cream salaatit kreem
salad dressing salsa li salaata
sale: is it for sale? da lil baya*?; **it's**
  not for sale mush lil baya*
sales clerk (*male*) baya*; (*female*)
  baya*a
salmon salamō
salt malH
salty: it's too salty da Hadi' awee
same zay; **one the same as this**

waaнid zay da; **the same again, please** waaнid tanee lowsamaнt; **have a good time — same to you** wa't sa*yeed — wa enta; **it's all the same to me** kuloo zay ba*dō; **thanks all the same** shukran

sand raml

sandals sanduhl; **a pair of sandals** sanduhl

sandstorm *aasifa ramlaya

sandwich 'sandwich'; **a cheese sandwich** 'sandwich' gibnuh; **felafel sandwich** 'sandwich' ta*amaya

sandy ramlee; **a sandy beach** bilaѕн ramlee

sanitary napkins/towels fewot saнaya

sarcastic mohazza'

sardines sardeen

satisfactory: this is not satisfactory da mıyuhrdeesh

Saturday yum e-sabt

sauce salsa

saucepan нala

saucer taba' fingāl

Saudi (man, adjective) sa*oodee; (woman) sa*oodaya

Saudi Arabia e-so*daya

sauna 'sauna'

sausage soogo'

sauté potatoes bataatis sōtay

save (life) uhnkuhz

savo(u)ry (noun) fateн li shaнaya

say: how do you say ... in Arabic? izzay ti'ool ... bil *arabee?; **what did you say?** olt ay?; **what did he say?** hoowa al ay?; **I said ... ana olt ...;** **he said ...** hoowa al ...; **I wouldn't say no** (yes please) lowsamaнt

scald: he's scalded himself hoowa нaнa' nafsoo

scarf (for neck) talfeeнa; (for head) asharb

scarlet aнmar zēhee

scenery manzuhr

scent (perfume) reeнa

schedule gadwel

scheduled flight reнla *adaya

school madrassa; (university) koolaya;

I'm still at school ana lessa fil madrassa

science *ılm

scissors: a pair of scissors ma'ass

scooter (motor scooter) 'scooter'

scorching: it's really scorching (weather) dee нarr fazee-a* awee

score: what's the score? e-nateega ay?

scorpion *a'ruhb

scotch (whisky) 'whisky'

Scotch tape (tm) shireet laz' sulōfān

Scotland eskotlanda

Scottish eskotlandee

scrambled eggs bayd ma'lee

scratch (noun) khadsh; **it's only a scratch** da khadsh baseet

scream (verb) sarakh

screw (noun) moosmarr alawawz

screwdriver mafak

scrubbing brush (for hands) forshit dawaafır; (for floors) forshit balaat

scruffy (appearance, hotel) mush nedeef; (person) mush nazeeh

scuba diving 'scuba diving'

sea baнr; **by the sea** ganb el baнr

sea air nismit el baнr

seafood samak

seafood restaurant mat*am asmak

seafront wag-hit el baнr; **on the seafront** *ala wag-hit el baнr

seagull noruhs

search (verb) fatish; **I searched everywhere** fatisht fee kuloo нetta

search party fer'it tafteesh

seashell suhduhfa

seasick: I feel seasick нassis bidookha; **I get seasick** baнass bidowaraan

seaside: by the seaside ganb el bilaѕн; **let's go to the seaside** yalla nerooн lil bilaѕн

season moosim; **in the high season** fil moosim; **in the low season** mush fil moosim

seasoning tawēbil

seat korsee; **is this anyone's seat?** нad a*ıd hena?

seat belt нezamil korsee; **do you have to wear a seat belt?** lezim testa*mil

el Hezam?
sea urchin onfid el baHr
seaweed *oshb baHree
secluded mon*azil
second (*adjective*) e-tanee; (*of time*)
sanya; **just a second!** estanna
shwIya!; **can I have a second helping?** mumkin tanee?
second class (*travel*) daraga tania
second-hand moosta*mil
secret (*noun*) sirr
secretary sekretēra (*f*)
sedative moosakin
see shēf; **I didn't see it** ana
mashuftoohoosh; **have you seen
my husband?** shuft goozee?; **I saw
him this morning** ana shuftoo e-
subHaya; **can I see the manager?**
mumkin ashoof el modeer?; **see you
tonight!** ashoofak bil layl!; **can I
see?** mumkin aboss?; **oh, I see** (*I
understand*) Iwa; **will you see to it?**
(*arrange it*) mumkin terratibboo?
seldom nēdir
self-catering apartment sha'a
mafroosha
self-service khedma zātaya
sell be-a*; **do you sell ...?** betbee-a*
...?; **will you sell it to me?** mumkin
tebe-a*hālee?
sellotape (*tm*) shireet laz' sulōfān
send ba*at; **I want to send this to
England** *a-Iyiz aba*at da lingilterra;
I'll have to send this food back
lezim araga* el akli da
senior: Mr Ahmed senior aHmed el
kebeer
senior citizen *agooz
sensational (*holiday, experience etc*)
momtaz
sense: I have no sense of direction
ma*andeesh fikra *an el itigahat; **it
doesn't make sense** da maloosh
ma*ana
sensible (*person*) *a'il; (*idea*) kwIyis
sensitive (*person, skin*) Hassēs
sentimental *aatifee
separate monfasil; **can we have
separate bills?** mumkin tefsil el

fawateer?
separately: we're paying separately
kuloo waaHHid HIedfa* li nafsoo;
we're travel(l)ing separately kuloo
waaHid HIsēfir li waHdō
September sibtimbuhr
septic ma*afin
serious (*person*) guhd; (*situation,
problem, illness*) khoteer; **I'm serious**
ana bakallim guhd; **you can't be
serious!** inta bit-huhzuhr!; **is it serious, doctor?** da khoteer, ya doktor?
seriously: seriously ill *Iyān awee
servant khadam
service: the service was excellent el
khedma kanit momtāza; **could we
have some service, please!** mumkin
tēkhud e-tuhluhb lowsamaHt?;
church service suhla fil kineesa; **the
car needs a service** el *arabaya
meHtaga kashf *am
service charge (*in restaurant*) rasm el
khedma
service station maHattit benzeen
serviette foota
set: it's time we were setting off el
mafrood eHna kunna mashyeen
delwa'tee
set menu kImit to*aam moHadadda
settle up: can we settle up now?
mumkin nedfa* delwa'tee?
several keteer
sew khIyat; **could you sew this back
on?** mumkin tekhIyat da?
sex (*sexual intercourse*) gins
sexy moghree
shade: in the shade fi dil
shadow khayēl
shake: let's shake hands yalla
nesallim
shallow (*water*) mush ghaweet
shame: what a shame! yādil *ar!
shampoo (*noun*) shamboo; **can I have
a shampoo and set?** ana *Iza
shamboo wi tessreeH
share (*verb: room, table etc*) shērik; **let's
share the cost** yalla nishērik el
fatoora
shark samak ersh

sharp (knife) Hamee; (taste) Hareef; (pain) shedeed

shattered: I'm shattered (very tired) ana ta*ban awee

shave: I need a shave ana meHtag aHla' da'nee; **can you give me a shave?** mumkin teHle' da'nee?

shaver makanit Hila'a

shaving brush forshit Hila'a

shaving foam 'cream' Hila'a

shaving point bareeza li makanit el Hila'a

shaving soap sabōn Hila'a

shawl shēl

she haya; **is she here?** haya hena?; **is she a friend of yours?** haya saHibituhk?; **she's not English** haya mush ingileezaya; see page 106

sheep kharoof

sheet (on bed) millaya; (of paper) safHa; (of glass etc) lōH

sheikh shaykh

shelf ruhf

shell suhduhfa

shellfish suhduhfa

sherry 'sherry'

shingles marad el Hazba

ship safeena; **by ship** bi safeena

shirt amees

shit! ela*na!

shock (surprise) suhdma; **I got an electric shock from the ...** ana etkaharabt min ...

shock-absorber musa*adeen

shocking (behaviour, prices, custom etc) fazee-a*

shoe fardit gazma; **my shoes** gazmetee; **a pair of shoes** gazma

shoelaces roobaat gazma

shoe polish warneesh

shop maHal; (small, local) dokkān (f)

shopping: I'm going shopping rIaH ashteree Haggēt

shop window batreenit el maHal

shore (of sea, lake) shuht

short (person, time, journey) ōsIyar; **it's only a short distance** mush bay*eeda

short-change: you've short-changed me inta iditnee el feloos na'sa

short circuit dIra ōsIyara

shortcut taree' mokhtassir

shorter/shortest a'suhr

shorts short; (underwear) koolot

should: what should I do? *amil ay?; **he shouldn't be long** hoowa zamānoo gay; **you should have told me** el malfrood ennak oltillee

shoulder kitf

shoulder blade *admit kitāf

shout (verb) za*'

show: could you show me? mumkin toowareenee?; **does it show?** da bayn?; **we'd like to go to a show** *Izeen nerooH nitfaruhg *ala este*raad

shower (in bathroom) dōsh; **with shower** bee dōsh

showercap bonnay

show-off: don't be a show-off matitla*ash feeha awee

shrimps gambaree

shrine duhreeH

shrink: it's shrunk da kash

shut (verb) afal; **when do you shut?** biti'fil emta?; **when do they shut?** biyi'filoo emta?; **it was shut** kan afil; **I've shut myself out** el bab eta'fil wanna barra; **shut up!** ekhrus!; (more polite) oskut!

shutter (on camera) monazim fatHet el *adessa; (on window) sheesh

shy khagool

sick (ill) *Iyān; **I think I'm going to be sick** (vomit) ana Hassis ennee Hatrush

side gamb; (in game) faree'; **at the side of the road** *ala gamb e-taree'; **the other side of town** fee akhr el medeena

side lights e-noor el waatee

side salad salaata

side street shari*a gānebee

sidewalk raseef

sidewalk café ahwa

siesta raHa

sight: the sights of ... monaazeer el ...

sightseeing: sightseeing tour gowla see-aнaya; **we're going sightseeing** rıнeen fee gowla see-aнaya
sign (*roadsign etc*) ishaara; (*written character*) ramz; **where do I sign?** uнmdee fayn?
signal: he didn't give a signal (*driver, cyclist*) hoowa madēsh ishaara
signature emda
signpost yafta
silence hidoo'
silencer *albit e-shakmān
silk нareer
silly (*person, thing to do etc*) sakheef; **that's silly!** da sakheef!
silver (*noun*) faada; (*adjective*) fidee
silver foil wara' fidee
similar zay
simple (*easy*) sahl
Sinai Peninsula seena
since: since yesterday min embarraн; **since we got here** min sa*ıt mageena hena
sincere mokhlis
sing ghenē
singer moghenee
single: a single room ōda lee waaнid; **a single to ...** tazkara lee ...; **I'm single** ana *azib
sink (*in kitchen*) нōd; **it sank** gher'it
sir effendee; **excuse me, sir** lowsamaнt yaffendee
sirloin 'steak'
sister okht; **my sister** okhtee
sister-in-law: my sister-in-law (*wife's sister*) okht miraatee; (*husband's sister*) okht goozee
sit: may I sit here? mumkin a*ood hena?; **is anyone sitting here?** fee нad hena?
situation mowkif
size нagm; (*of clothes*) ma'ass; **do you have any other sizes?** *andak ma'assat tania?
sketch (*noun*) 'sketch'
ski (*noun: for waterskiing*) 'ski'
skid: I skidded ana etzaнla't
skin gild
skin-diving 'skin diving'; **I'm going**

skin-diving ana rıaн 'skin diving'
skinny naнeef awee
skirt goonilla
skull gomgomma
sky samma
sleep nam; **I can't sleep** mush a'dar anam; **did you sleep well?** nimt kwıyis?; **I need a good sleep** ana meнtag noom keteer
sleeper (*rail: whole train*) atr e-noom
sleeping bag kees linoom
sleeping car (*rail*) *arabayit noom
sleeping pill нabba minawimma
sleepy (*person*) na*asēn; (*weather, day*) minowim; (*town*) hadia; **I'm feeling sleepy** ana na*asēn
sleeve kum
slice (*noun*) нetta
slide (*photography*) 'slide'
slim (*adjective*) naнeef; **I'm slimming** ana ba*mil resнeem
slip (*under dress*) amees taнtanee; **I slipped** (*on pavement etc*) etzaнla't
slipped disc inzilluhk ghadroofee
slippers ship ship
slippery mizaнla'; **it's slippery** mizнla'a
slow batee'; **slow down!** (*driving*) hadee e-sor*a!; (*speaking*) ēhda!
slowly baraнa; **could you say it slowly?** mumkin ti'oloo baraнa?; **very slowly** baraнa awee
small sooghıar
smaller/smallest uhsghar
small change fakka
smallpox el gudaree
smart (*clothes*) uhneek
smashing (*holiday, time, food etc*) gameel
smell: there's a funny smell fee reeнa ghereeba; **what a lovely smell!** reeнa нelwa awee!; **it smells** (*smells bad*) reeнa weнsha
smile (*verb*) ebtasuhm
smoke (*noun*) dokhan; **do you smoke?** bidakhan?; **do you mind if I smoke?** mumkin adakhan?; **I don't smoke** mabadakhansh
smooth (*surface*) na*ım

snack: I'd just like a snack ana *a-
ıyiz tuhsbeera
snackbar 'cafeteria'
snake te*aban
sneakers gazma kawetsh
snob mitkuhbuhr
snorkel 'snorkel'
snow (noun) talg
so: it's so hot Harr awee; it was so
beautiful! kan gameel awee!; not so
fast mush bisora*a; thank you so
much shukran gazeelan; it wasn't —
it was so! la' makensh — ıwa kan;
so am I ana kamēn; so do I ana
kamēn; how was it? — so-so ay el
akhbar? — nus-oo-nus
soaked: I'm soaked ana mablool
soaking solution (for contact lenses)
maHloof lituhndeef
soap sabōn
soap-powder mas-Hoo' gheseel
sober (not drunk) razeen; (serious) gad
soccer kora kuhduhm
sock fardit sharab; socks sharab
socket (electrical) bareeza
soda (water) 'soda'
sofa kanaba
soft (material etc) na*ım
soft drink mashroob gheer kaнolee
soldier *askaree
sole (of shoe) na*l; (of foot) batn e-rigl;
could you put new soles on these?
mumkin terakib na*l gedeed lee
dōl?
solid gāmid
Somalia e-somaal
Somalian somaalee
some: may I have some water?
mumkin shwıyit mıya?; do you have
some matches? ma*ak kabreet?; (in
a shop) *andak kabreet?; that's some
drink! da mashroob tamam awee!;
some of them ba*dōhum; can I
have some? (small amount of cheese
etc) mumkin akhud shwıya?; can I
have some (oranges etc) mumkin
(bortoo'aan etc)?; see page 102
somebody, someone Had
something Haga; something to drink

Haga ashrabha
sometime: sometime this afternoon
ba*d e-dohr
sometimes aнeeyēnan
somewhere: somewhere in the room
fil ōda; I put it down somewhere
ana Hatēttoo fee maken
son ibn; my son ibnee
song oghnaya
son-in-law gooz bint; my son-in-law
gooz bintee
soon Hālan; I'll be back soon Harga*
bisora*; as soon as you can bee-
asra* mıyumkin
sore: it's sore bitewga*
sore throat: I have a sore throat
andee waga fi zor
sorry: (I'm) sorry asif; sorry? (didn't
understand) na*m?
sort: what sort of ...? ay nōa* ...?; a
different sort of ... nōa* tanee min
...; will you sort it out? mumkin
teнeloo?
soup shorba
sour (taste) haamid
source of the Nile mamba* e-neel
south ganoob; to the south lil ganoob
South Africa ganoob afrikia
South African (adjective, person) min
ganoob afrikia
southeast el ganoob e-shar'ee; to the
southeast lil ganoob e-shar'ee
southwest el ganoob el gharbee; to
the southwest lil ganoob el gharbee
souvenir tizkaar
spa yanbooa*
space heater sakhēn kaharaba
spade (tool) ma*za'a
spades (cards) buhstōnee
Spain esbania
spanner muftaH ingileezee
spare part kitta*it gheeyar
spare tyre/tire *agala estebn
spark(ing) plug booSHeehat
speak: do you speak English?
bitikallim ingileezee?; I don't speak
... ana mabakallimsh ...; can I speak
to ...? mumkin akallim ...?; speaking
(on telephone) bikallim

special khosoosee; **nothing special** *adee

specialist mokhtuhs

special(i)ty: the special(i)ty of the house akl maHallee

spectacles nuhdaara

speed (*noun*) sora*a; **he was speeding** hoowa kan saye' bisora*a

speedboat luhnsh

speed limit e-sora*a el *ozma

speedometer *adad e-sora*a

spend saraf; **I've spent all my money** saraft kul feloosee

sphinx abul hōl

spice booharr

spicy: it's very spicy Hāmee awee

spider *ankaboot

splendid (*very good*) momtaz

splint (*for broken limb*) gabeera

splinter (*in finger*) shazee-a

splitting: I've got a splitting headache *andee suda* shedeed

spoke (*in wheel*) silk

sponge safinga

spoon ma*le'a

sport reeyaada

sport(s) jacket sHakit

spot (*on face etc*) dimil; **will they do it on the spot?** HIya*miloo fee wa'taha?

sprain: I've sprained my ... ana lawayt ...

spray (*for hair*) bakhēkhēh

spring (*season*) e-rabee-a*; (*of car, seat*) sosat

square (*in town*) midan; **ten square metres** *ashara mitr mooruhba*

squash (*sport*) 'squash'

stain (*noun: on clothes*) bo'a*a

stairs sallēlim (*f*)

stale (*bread, taste*) mush taaza

stall: the engine keeps stalling el mator bee'ata*

stalls (*in theatre*) saala

stamp (*noun*) taabea*; **a stamp for England, please** taabea* lingilterra, lowsamaHt

stand: I can't stand ... (*can't tolerate*) mush a'dar atHāmil ...

standard (*adjective*) mustowa

standby 'waiting list'

star (*in sky*) nigma; (*person*) nigm

start (*noun*) el beedaya; **when does the film start?** el film beeyebda' emta?; **the car won't start** el *arabaya mabidorsh

starter (*of car*) el marsh; (*food*) fateH lil shahaya

starving: I'm starving ana mayit min el goo-a*

state (*in country*) willaya; **the States** (*USA*) amreeka

station (*train*) maHattit e-sikka el Hadeed; (*bus*) mow'af el ōtōbeesēt

statue timsēl

stay: we enjoyed our stay eHna enbassuhtna awee; **where are you staying?** inta nezil fayn?; **I'm staying at ...** ana nazil fee ...; **I'd like to stay another week** *a-Iyiz a*od isboo*a tanee; **I'm staying in tonight** ana mush khērig elleelādee

steak 'steak'

steal sere'; **my bag has been stolen** shantitee etsere'it

steep (*hill*) Hād

steering e-drikseeyōn; **the steering is slack** e-drikseeyōn bee fawit

steering wheel itar e-drikseeyōn

step (*in front of house etc*) buhsta

stereo 'stereo'

sterling estirleenee

steward (*on plane*) modeef

stewardess modeefa

sticking plaster blastar

sticky: it's sticky da milaza'

sticky tape shireet laza'

still: I'm still waiting ana lessa mistanee; **will you still be open?** Hatkoon lessa fateH?; **it's still not right** da lessa mush tamem; **that's still better** da aHsen; **keep still!** ō'af sēbit

sting: a bee sting arsit naHla; **I've been stung** ana et'aruhst

stink (*noun*) reeHa weHsha; **it stinks** reeHtoo waHesh awee

stockings sharab feellay

stolen masroo'; **my wallet's been**

stolen maнfuhztee etsara'it
stomach me*ada; **do you have something for an upset stomach?** *andak нaga lee waga* el me*ada?
stomach-ache maghas
stone (rock) нaguhr; see page 118
stop (bus stop) maнattit ōtōbees; **which is the stop for ...?** fayn el maнatta lee ...?; **please, stop here** (to taxi driver etc) hena lowsamaнt; **do you stop near ...?** bitō'af orıyib min ...?; **stop doing that!** buhtuhl da!
stopover 'transit'
store (shop) maнal; (small, local) dokkān (f)
stor(e)y (of building) dor
storm *asifa
story (tale) kissa
stove forn
straight (road etc) mustakeem; **it's straight ahead** *alatool; **straight away** fowran; **a straight whisky** 'whisky' li waнdo
straighten: can you straighten things out? (sort things out) mumkin tefuhdee ishkal?
strange (odd) ghereeb; (unknown) ghereeb
stranger ghereeb; **I'm a stranger here** ana mush min hena
strap (on watch) ōstayk; (on dress, on suitcase) нēzam
strawberry farowla
streak (in hair) mashēt; **could you put streaks in?** mumkin mashēt fi sha*r?
stream magra
street shari*a; **on the street** fi shari*a
street café ahwa
streetcar tromı
streetmap khareetit toro'
strep throat waga* zor
strike (noun) idraab; **are they on strike?** fee idraab?; **they're on strike** modribeen *an e-shoghl
string doobaara; **have you got some string?** (in a shop) *andak doobaar?; (to a person) ma*ak doobaar?
striped ma'allim
stroke: he's just had a stroke gatlō

zabнa sadraya
stroll: let's go for a stroll yalla nuhkhrug nitmasha
stroller (for babies) *arabit tefl
strong (person, voice) shedeed; (taste, curry) нāmee; (drink) morakaz
stroppy (official, waiter) *ınadee
stuck maznoo'; **the key's stuck** el muftaн etzana'
student (male) taalib; (female) taalibba
stuffed vine leaves wara' *ınab
stupid ghebee; **that's stupid** da ghebē'
sty(e) (in eye) ramad нobaybee
subtitles targamma
suburb dawaнee
subway (underground) nafa'
successful: were you successful? inta etwafa't?
Sudan e-soodan
Sudanese (man, adjective) soodānee; (woman) soodanaya
suddenly fag'a
sue: I intend to sue нarfa* da*wa
suede shamwa
Suez Canal konat e-seewis
sugar sukar; **without sugar** sēda
sugar cane asab
suggest: what do you suggest? ra'yak ay?
suit (noun) badla; **it doesn't suit me** mabit nasibneesh; **it suits you** нelwa *aleek; **that suits me fine** da yirdeenee awee
suitable (time, place) monāsib
suitcase shantit safar
sulk: he's sulking hoowa mibowiz
sultan sultaan
sultana (wife of sultan) sultaana
sultry (weather, climate) rōtooba *alee-a
summer si-if; **in the summer** fi si-if
sun shams (f); **in the sun** fi shams; **out of the sun** fi dil; **I've had too much sun** ana нassis bee darbit shams
sunbathe etshamis
sunblock (cream) 'cream' duhd e-shams
sunburn lafнet shams

sunburnt maнroo' min e-shams
Sunday yum el нad
sunglasses naddara shamsaya
sun lounger (*chair*) кorsee lil bilasн
sunny: if it's sunny low mishamissa; **a sunny day** yum mishamis
sunrise shiroo' e-shams
sun roof (*in car*) sa'f motaнarig
sunset ghroob e-shams
sunshade shamsaya
sunshine shoo*a* e-shams
sunstroke darbit shams
suntan suнmar min e-shams
suntan lotion loshan li shams
suntanned ismar min e-shams; **I'm suntanned** ana esmareet min e-shams
suntan oil zayt li shams
sun worshipper *abeed e-shams
super (*time, holiday*) lazeez; (*person*) momtaz; **super!** momtaz!
superb (*buildings, sunsets, view*) rowa*a
supermarket 'supermarket'
supper *asha
supplement (*extra charge*) rasm idaafee
suppose: I suppose so a*tuhkid kedda
suppository om*a
sure: I'm sure ana muta'akid; **are you sure?** inta muta'akid?; **he's sure** hoowa muta'akid; **sure!** o kay!
surf 'surf'
surfboard 'surfboard', loн enzilaak
surfing: I want to go surfing ana *a-ıyiz 'surfing'
surname ism el ıayla
surprise (*noun*) mufag'a
surprising: that's not surprising da kan muta wokea*
suspension (*of car*) soset

swallow (*verb*) bala*
swearword shiteema
sweat (*verb*) *arı'; (*noun*) *ara'; **covered in sweat** *ar'en
sweater soo-wetuhr
sweatshirt fanilla
Sweden e-sweed
sweet (*taste*) нelw; (*noun: dessert*) нelw
sweets нalawee-at
swelling waram
sweltering: it's sweltering dee нarr awee
swerve: I had to swerve (*when driving*) etuhrit aнowid bisora*a
swim (*verb*) *am; **I'm going for a swim** ana гıнa a*-oom; **do you want to go for a swim?** inta *a-ıyiz teroон te*-oom?; **I can't swim** ma*arafsh a*-oom
swimming sibaнa; **I like swimming** ana baнebb e-sibaнa
swimming costume mayo нareemee
swimming pool нammem sibaнa
swimming trunks mayo rigalee
Swiss swisree
switch (*noun*) muftaн; **could you switch it on?** (*radio, TV, lights*) mumkin tewal*ow?; (*engines, machines*) mumkin tesheghelha?; **could you switch it off?** (*radio, TV, lights*) mumkin tetfeeh?; (*engines, machines*) mumkin tibatuнlha?
Switzerland swissra
swollen werim
swollen glands ghodad werma
sympathy *aatf
synagogue ma*abad yahoodee
synthetic estina*ı
Syria suree-a
Syrian (*man, adjective*) sooree; (*woman*) sooraya

T

table tarabayza; **a table for two** tarabayza litneen; **at our usual table** *and e-tarabayza el mo*atēda
tablecloth mafrash tarabayza
table tennis bing bong
table wine nebeet
tactful (*person*) labik
tailback (*of traffic*) taboor *arabeeyaat
tailor tarzee
take khad; **will you take this to room 12?** mumkin tekhud da lee ōda itnaashar?; **will you take me to the airport?** mumkin tekhudnee lil mataar?; **do you take credit cards?** bitekhud 'credit card'?; **OK, I'll take it** 'OK' Hakhdō; **how long does it take?** bitekhud ad ay?; **it'll take 2 hours** Hawalee sa*atayn; **is this seat taken?** fee Had a*ad hena?; **I can't take too much sun** ma*adarsh a*ood keteer fi shams; **will you take this back, it's broken** mumkin teraga*da, da maksoor?; **could you take it in at the side?** (*dress, jacket*) mumkin tikassim el ginab shwiya?; **when does the plane take off?** e-tiyara ma*adha emta?; **can you take a little off the top?** (*to hairdresser*) mumkin te'oss shwiya sooghiyara min fo'?
talcum powder budrit talk
talk (*verb*) etkallim
tall (*person*) taweel; (*building*) *alee
taller/tallest atwuhl
tampax 'tampax' (*tm*)
tampons 'tampax' (*tm*)
tan (*noun*) samar min e-shams; **I want to get a good tan** ana *a-iyiz asmar min e-shams
tank (*of car*) 'tank'
tap Hanafaya

tape (*for cassette*) 'cassette'; (*sticky*) shireet laza'
tape measure mazoora
tape recorder rekordar
taste (*noun*) ta*m; **can I taste it?** mumkin adoo'oo?; **it has a peculiar taste** ta*moo ghereeb; **it tastes very nice** ta*moo Helw awee; **it tastes revolting** ta*moo waHesh awee
taxi taks; **taxi!** taks, taks!; **will you get me a taxi?** mumkin tegiblee taks?
taxi-driver sawē' taks
taxi rank, taxi stand mow'af takseeyet
tea (*drink*) shay; **tea for two please** shay litneen lowsamaHt; **could I have a cup of tea?** mumkin kubayit shay?
teabag kees shay
teach: could you teach me? mumkin te*alimnee?; **could you teach me Arabic?** mumkin te*alimnee *arabee?
teacher (*male*) mōdaris; (*female*) mōdarissa
team faree'
teapot baraad shay
tea towel foota
teenager (*male*) moraahik; (*female*) moraahikka
teetotal: he's teetotal hoowa mabyeshrabsh khaalis
telegram teleghraaf; **I want to send a telegram** ana *a-iyiz aba*t teleghraaf
telephone telefōn; **can I make a telephone call?** mumkin asta*mil e-telefōn?; **could you talk to him for me on the telephone?** mumkin tekallimoo fi telefōn *alashēnee?
telephone box/booth kabeenit telefōn

telephone directory daleel telefōnet
telephone number rakuhm e-telefōn;
what's your telephone number?
nimrit telefōnak kam?
telephoto lens *adaset tuhsweer
television teleevizyōn; **I'd like to
watch television** ana *a-ıyiz atfaruhg
*ala e-teleevizyōn; **is the match on
television?** el muhtsh fi teleevizyōn?
tell: could you tell him ...? mumkin
ti'olloo ...?
temperature (*weather*) dargit el
Harara; (*fever*) Homma; **he has a
temperature** *andoo Homma
temple (*religious*) ma*abad; **Hatshepsut's temple** dē-ir el baHaree
temporary mo'uhkuht
tenant (*of apartment*) musta'gir
tennis 'tennis'
tennis ball korit 'tennis'
tennis court mala*b 'tennis'; **can we
use the tennis court?** mumkin
nista*mil mala*b e-'tennis'?
tennis racket muhdruhb 'tennis'
tent khayma
term (*at university, school*) fasl
terminus (*rail*) mow'af
terrace varanduh; **on the terrace** fil
varanduh
terrible (*weather, food, accent*) fazee-a*
terrific (*weather, food, teacher*) momtaz
testicle khisya
than min; **smaller than** uhsghar min;
bigger than uhkbar min
thanks, thank you shukran; **thank
you very much** shukran gazeelan;
thank you for everything shukran
*ala kulla Haga; **no thanks** la'
mutsheka
that: that woman e-sittee dee; **that
man** e-raagil da; **that one** da/dee; **I
hope that ...** atmana en ...; **that's
perfect** da tamem; **that's strange** da
ghereeb; **is that ...?** da ...?; **that's it**
(*right*) saH!; **is it that expensive?**
da ghēlee?; *see pages 106, 107*
the el; *see page 102*
theater, theatre masraH
their: their address *ınwanhum;

their house bayt-hum; *see page 105*
theirs bita*hum; *see page 108*
them humma; **for them** leehum; **with
them** ma*ahum; **I gave it to them**
ana eddit-hulhum; **who? — them**
meen? — humma; *see page 106*
then ba*dayn
there hinak; **over there** hinak; **up
there** fo'; **is there ...?** fee ...?; **are
there ...?** fee ...?; **there is ...** fee ...;
there are ... fee ...; **there you are**
(*giving something*) itfuhduhl
thermal spring *ın sukhna
thermometer tuhrmomituhr
thermos flask tuhrmos
thermostat (*in car*) thuhrmōstat
these dōl; **can I have these?** mumkin
dōl?; *see pages 106, 107*
they humma; **are they ready?** humma
gahzeen?; **are they coming?** humma
gayeen?; *see page 106*
thick tekheen; (*stupid*) ghebee
thief Haraamee
thigh fakhd
thin roofıya*
thing Haga; **have you seen my
things?** shuft Hagtee?; **first thing in
the morning** (*very early*) e-subH
badree
think fakuhr; **what do you think?** ay
ra'yak?; **I think so** *ala mazon; **I
don't think so** maftikersh; **I'll think
about it** Hafuhkuhr fee
third-class darga talta
third party insurance ta'meen *ala
el gheer
thirsty: I'm thirsty ana *atshaan
this: this hotel el fondō' da; **this
town** el medeena dee; **this one**
(*masculine noun*) da; (*feminine noun*)
dee; **this is my wife** dee miraatee;
this is my favo(u)rite café dee
ahwitee el mifuhdulla; **is this yours?**
da bita*ak?; *see pages 106, 107*
those dōl; **not these, those** mush dōl,
dōl; *see pages 106, 107*
thread (*noun*) alawawz
throat zor
throat lozenges bastilya

throttle (*on motorbike*) khēni
through: does it go through Tanta? beey*adee *ala tuhntuh?; Monday through Friday min yum el itneen lee yum el gom*a; straight through the city centre *alatool fee nus el balad
through train atr tawaalee
throw (*verb*) rama; don't throw it away matermihash; I'm going to throw up ana нatrush
thumb e-sooba* el kebeer
thumbtack daboos
thunder (*noun*) ra*ad
thunderstorm bar' wi ra*ad
Thursday yum el khamees
ticket (*for bus, train, plane, cinema, cloakroom*) tazkara
ticket office (*bus, rail*) maktab e-tazēkir
tie (*noun: around neck*) garafatta
tight (*clothes etc*) dιye'; the waist is too tight el wist dιye' awee
tights sharab fee-lay
time wa't; what's the time? e-sa*a kam?; at what time do you close? bite'fil e-sa*a kam?; there's not much time mafeesh wa't; for the time being delwa'tee; from time to time min wa't lee tanee; right on time *alel ma*ad bizobt; this time el maraadee; last time el mara ellee fatit; next time el mara e-gaya; four times arba*a maraat; have a good time! atmanna lak wa't sa*yeed; *see page 116*
timetable gadwil el mo*a-ıd
tin (*can*) *alba
tinfoil wara' fidee
tin-opener fateнit *ılab
tint (*verb: hair*) lowin
tiny sooghıyar awee
tip (*to waiter etc*) ba'sheesh
tire (*for car*) kawetsh *arabaya
tired ta*aben; I'm tired ana ta*aben
tiring mot*ıb
tissues kliniks
to: to Egypt/to England li masr/lingilterra; to London lee 'london';

to the airport lil mataar; here's to you! (*toast*) fee saнetuhk!; *see page 116*
toast (*bread*) 'toast'; (*drinking*) nakhb
tobacco dokhēn
tobacconist, tobacco store maнal sagayar
today e-naharda; today week isboo-a* min e-naharda
toe sooba* rigl
toffee 'toffee'
together ma*aba*d; we're together eнna ma*aba*d; can we pay together? mumkin nitfa* fatoora waнda?
toilet tawalet; where's the toilet? fayn e-tawalet?; I have to go to the toilet ana lēzim arooн li tawalet; she's in the toilet haya fi tawalet
toilet paper wara' tawalet
toilet water kolonya
tomato oota
tomato juice *aseer oota
tomato ketchup 'ketchup'
tomb ma'barra
tomorrow bukra; tomorrow morning bukra e-subн; tomorrow afternoon bukra e-dohr; tomorrow evening bukra bil layl; the day after tomorrow ba*d bukra; see you tomorrow ashoofak bukra
ton tin; *see page 118*
tongue lissan
tonic (*water*) mιya ma*danaya
tonight elleelādee, el layla dee; not tonight mush elleelādee
tonsillitis eltihab el lēwaz
tonsils el lēwaz
too (*excessively*) awee; (*also*) kamēn; too hot нarr awee; too much keteer awee; me too ana kamēn; I'm not feeling too good ana mush kwιyis
tooth sinna
toothache waga* seenan
toothbrush forshit seenan
toothpaste ma*goon asnan
top: on top of ... fo' el ...; on top of the car fo' el *arabaya; on the top floor fil dor el akheer; at the top

fo'; **at the top of the tower** fo' el
borg; **top quality** sanf momtaz;
bikini top beekeenee
torch bataraya
total (*noun*) magmoo-a*
touch (*verb*) lamas; **let's keep in
touch** dawim el gawabēt
tough (*meat etc*) gamid; **tough luck!**
ma*alesh!
tour (*noun*) gowla; **is there a tour of
...?** fee gowla lee ...?
tour guide morshid seeyaнee
tourist sayaн
tourist information office maktab e-
seeyaнa
tourist police bolees e-seeyaнa
touristy seeyeнee; **somewhere not so
touristy** makan mush seeyeнee
tour operator maktab seeyaнa
tow: can you give me a tow? mumkin
teshadnee?
**toward(s): Tanta is toward(s) Alex-
andria** tuhntuh teega iskindraya;
**I'm travel(l)ing toward(s) Alex-
andria** ana misāfir iskindraya
towel foota
town medeena; **in town** fee nus el
balad; **which bus goes into town?**
ōtōbees kam beerooн li nus el
balad?; **we're staying just out of
town** eнna sekneen fee dawaнee el
medeena
town hall mabna el moнafzuh
tow rope нabl
toy le*aba
trachoma ramuhd нobaybee
track suit tiring
traditional aslee; **a traditional
Egyptian meal** akla masraya; **a
traditional restaurant** mata*m
shar'ee; **traditional costume** zay
masree aslee
traffic muhroor (*f*)
traffic cop *askaree muhroor
traffic jam zaнmit muhroor
traffic light(s) isharaat el muhroor
trailer (*for carrying tent etc*) ma'toora
train atr; **when's the next train to ...?**
emta ma*ad el atr lil ...; **by train** bil

atr
trainers (*shoes*) gazma kawetsh
train station maнattit atr
tram tromi
tramp (*person*) raнaal
tranquillizers mohadee
transfer desk maktab e-taнweelēt
transformer (*electrical*) tarans
transistor (*radio*) radee-ō tranzistor
transit lounge (*at airport*) saalit e-
transit
translate tergim; **could you translate
that?** mumkin tetargim da?
translation targamma
translator motargim
transmission (*of car*) na'l el нarikuh
travel safuhr; **we're travel(l)ing
around** eнna binit gowil
travel agent wikālit suhfuhr
travel(l)er musēfir
traveller's cheque, traveler's check
sheek seeyaнee
tray sanaya
treasure kinooz (*f*)
tree shuhgara
tremendous momtaz
trendy (*person, clothes, restaurant*)
sнims
tribe kaabeela
tribesman waaнid min el kaabeela
tricky (*difficult*) sa*ab
trim: just a trim please (*to hairdresser*)
uhs buhseet lowsamaнt
trip (*journey*) reнla; **I'd like to go on
a trip to ...** ana *a-ιyiz atla* reнla
lee ...; **have a good trip** reнla
sa*yeeda
tripod (*for camera*) нamil bitalluht
rigool
tropical (*heat, climate*) istoo-wē'ee
trouble (*noun*) mashēkil; **I'm having
trouble with ...** ana *andee mashēkil
ma*a ...; **sorry to trouble you** asif lil
iz*ag
trousers bantalōn
trouser suit badla нareemee
truck looree
truck driver sawē' na'l
true нa'ee'ee; **that's not true** da mush

saн
trunk (*of car*) shanta; (*for belongings*) sandoo' нidoom
trunks (*swimming*) mayō rigālee
truth нa'ee'a; **it's the truth** dil нa'ee'a
try нawil; **please try** нawil lowsamaнt; **will you try for me?** mumkin teнawil *alashēnee?; **I've never tried it** (*food etc*) ana *omree magarabtoo; **can I have a try?** (*food*) mumkin adoo'oo?; (*at doing something*) mumkin agarab?; **may I try it on?** (*clothes*) mumkin a'eesoo
T-shirt amees nussa kom
tube (*for tyre*) etaar dakhilee
Tuesday yum e-talaat
tuition: I'd like tuition ana менtag te*aleem
tuna fish samak toona
tune (*noun*) laнn
Tunis toonis
Tunisia toonis
Tunisian (*man, adjective*) toonissee; (*woman*) toonisaya
tunnel nafa'
Turkey torkaya

turkey deek roomee
Turkish delight malban
turn: it's my turn now da dooree ana; **turn left** нowid shimēl; **where do we turn off?** naнowid fayn?; **can you turn the air-conditioning on?** mumkin teshaghel e-takeef?; **can you turn the air-conditioning off?** mumkin tetfee e-takeef?; **he didn't turn up** hoowa magesh
turning (*in road*) танweeda
TV teleevizyōn
tweezers mol'aat
twice maritayn; **twice as much** e-da*f
twin beds sireerayn
twin room ōda litneen
twins tow'am
twist: I've twisted my ankle ana lowayt ka*abee
type (*noun*) nōa*; **a different type of ...** nōa* tanee min ...
typewriter alakatba
typhoid тıfood
typical (*dish etc*) aslee; **that's typical!** da aslee!
tyre kawetsh

U

ugly (*person, building*) waнesh awee
ulcer orнa
Ulster irlanda e-shamalaya
umbrella shamsaya
uncle (*father's brother*) *am; (*mother's brother*) khel
uncomfortable (*chair etc*) mush moreeн
unconscious moghma *alay
under (*spatially*) танt; (*less than*) a'el min
underdone (*meat*) nīya
underground (*rail*) nafa'
underpants koolot
undershirt fanilla

understand: I don't understand mush fēhim; **I understand** fēhim; **do you understand?** inta fēhim?
underwear malābis dakhilaya
undo (*clothes*) khala*
uneatable: it's uneatable mayitakelsh
unemployed *aatil
unfair: that's unfair da mush *adl
unfortunately lee soo'el нuz
unfriendly mush нebbee
unhappy нazeen
unhealthy (*person, climate etc*) mush seнe
United Arab Emirates el emiraat
United States amreeka; **in the**

United States fee amreeka

university gama*a

unlimited mileage (*on hire car*) masĕfuh gheer maHdooda

unlock fataH; **the door was unlocked** el bab kan maftooH

unpack fak

unpleasant (*person, taste*) mush kwIyis

unpronounceable: it's unpronounceable mush a'dar a'ooloo

untie fak

until laHad; **until we meet again** (*said as parting words*) laHad mānit'ābil tanee; **not until Wednesday** mush abl yum el arba*

unusual shez

up fo'; **further up the road** ō'dam shwIya; **up there** fo'; **he's not up yet** (*not out of bed*) hoowa lessa mas-Heesh; **what's up?** (*what's wrong?*) fee ay?

upmarket (*restaurant, hotel, goods etc*)
ghĕlee

Upper Egypt wag iblee, (*colloquial word*) e-sIyeed

upset stomach waga* batn

upside down ma'loob

upstairs fo'

urgent mista*gil; **it's very urgent** da mōhim gidan gidan

urinary tract infection eltihab el masēna el bowlaya

us: with us ma*ana; **for us** *alashĕnna; *see page 106*

use (*verb*) esta*mil; **may I use ...?** mumkin asta*mil ...?; **may I use the phone?** mumkin e-telefōn?

used: I used to swim a lot ana kunt ba*owm keteer; **when I get used to the heat** lamma ēkhud *alel Harr

useful mōfeed

usual *adee; **as usual** zay el *ada

usually *adetan

U-turn dowaraan lil khalf

V

vacancy: do you have any vacancies? (*hotel*) fee ewad fadee-a?

vacation agĕzza; **we're here on vacation** eHna hena fee agĕzza

vaccination tuht *Iyeem

vacuum cleaner maknassa bil kaharaba

vacuum flask tuhrmos

vagina raHm

valid (*ticket etc*) salHa; **how long is it valid for?** salHa li'ad ay?

valley wĕdee

Valley of the Kings wĕdee el milook

valuable (*adjective*) sameen; **can I leave my valuables here?** mumkin aseeb momtallakaatee hena?

value (*noun*) eema

van *arabaya na'l

vanilla vanilla; **a vanilla ice cream** sHelaatee vanilla

varicose veins dawĕllee

variety show Haflit minawa*at

vary: it varies bitikh-telif

vase vaaza

vaudeville Haflit minawa*at

VD marad tanasollee

veal laHma kandooz

vegetables khōdar

vegetarian nabātee; **I'm a vegetarian** ana nabātee

veil Hegab

velvet ateefa

vending machine makanit baya*

ventilator tahwaya

very awee; **very hot** sukhn awee; **just a very little Arabic** *arabee mokassuhr awee; **I only speak a very little Arabic** batkallim *arabee

shwıya; **just a very little for me**
shwıya sooghıyara *alashēnee; **I like**
it very much ana baHebboo keteer
awee

vest (*under shirt*) fanilla; (*waistcoat*)
sideree

via *antuhree'; **via Cairo** *antuhree'
el kaheera

video (*noun*) 'video'

view manzar; **what a superb view!** da
manzar gameel awee!

viewfinder (*of camera*) zaabit el
manzar

villa villa

village kareeya

vine *ınab

vinegar khel

visa 'visa'

visibility (*for driving*) rō'ya

visit (*verb*) zar; **I'd like to visit ...** ana
*a-ıyiz azor ...; **come and visit us**
ebba te*ala zorna

vital: it's vital that ... da mōhim in ...

vitamins vitameen

vodka 'vodka'

voice sōt

voltage volt

vomit (*verb*) tarash; (*noun*) toraash

W

wafer (*with ice cream*) baskaweeta

waist wist

waistcoat sideree

wait estanna; **wait for me** estannēnee;
don't wait for me matistanneesh; **it**
was worth waiting for fe*alan kan
yistaHa' el intizar; **I'll wait until my**
wife comes ana Hastanna miraatee;
I'll wait a little longer Hastanna
shwıya kamen; **can you do it while**
I wait? mumkin ta*miloo wana
hena?; **wait a minute** estanna shwıya

waiter garsōn; **waiter!** lowsamaHt!

waiting room Hogrit el intizar

waitress garsōna; **waitress!**
lowsamaHt!

wake: will you wake me up at 6.30?
mumkin tessaHeenee e-sa*a sitta wa
nus?

Wales 'wales'

walk: let's walk there yalla nimshee;
is it possible to walk there?
mumkin atmashēha?; **I'll walk back**
Harga* mashee; **is it a long walk?**
haya masēfa too-weela?; **it's only a**
short walk da mush ba*yeed; **I'm**
going out for a walk ana kherig

atmasha; **let's take a walk around**
town yalla nitmasha fil balad

walking stick *okez

walkman (*tm*) kassit sooghıyar

wall Hayta

wallet maHfuhza

wander: I like just wandering
around ana baHebb atfaruhg

want: I want a ... (*said by man*) ana
*a-ıyiz ...; (*said by woman*) ana *a-ıza
...; **I don't want any** mush *a-ıyiz; **I**
want to go home ana *a-ıyiz arooH;
I don't want to mush *a-ıyiz; **he**
wants to ... hoowa *a-ıyiz ...; **what**
do you want? *a-ıyiz ay?

war Harb

ward (*in hospital*) *ambuhr

warm dēfee; **it's so warm today** e-
gow dēfee e-naharda; **I'm so warm**
ana dafeeyen awee

warning (*noun*) inzar

was: it was ... kan ...; **was it ...?** kan
...?; *see page 113*

wash (*verb*) ghesil; **I need a wash** ana
meHtag ashuhtuhf; **can you wash**
the car? mumkin teghsil el
*arabaya?; **can you wash these?**

mumkin teghsillee dōl?; **it'll wash
off** Hatitla* fil gheseel
washcloth foota
washer (*for bolt etc*) gilbuh, warda
washhand basin Hōd
washing (*clothes*) gheseel; **where can I
hang my washing?** anshur el gheseel
fayn?; **can you do my washing for
me?** mumkin teghsillee gheseelee?
washing machine ghasella
washing powder mas-Hoo' gheseel
washing-up: I'll do the washing-up
ana Haghsil el mowI-een
washing-up liquid se'il lighesl e-
soHoon
wasp duhboor
wasteful: that's wasteful da tabzeer
wastepaper basket salit el mohmeelet
watch (*wrist-*) sa*a; **will you watch
my things for me?** mumkin tekhud
bālak min Hagtee?; **I'll just watch**
ana Hatfaruhg bass; **watch out!**
Hasib!
watch strap ostayk sa*a
water mIya; **may I have some water?**
mumkin shwIyit mIya?
water-bottle ezāzit mIya
watercolo(u)r alwān mIya
waterpipe (*to smoke*) sheesha
waterproof (*adjective*) duhd el mIya
waterski: I'd like to learn to waterski
ana *a-Iyiz at*allim et-tazaHlo' *ala el
mIya
waterskiing 'waterskiing'
water sports reeyaddeeyaat ma'aya
water wheel sa'ya
wave (*in sea*) mooga
way: which way is it? fee ay e-teega?;
it's this way fil e-teega da; **it's that
way** fil e-teega da; **could you tell
me the way to ...?** mumkin te'ollee
e-taree' lil ...?; **is it on the way to
Alexandria?** da fi taree' iskindraya?;
you're blocking the way inta sēdid
e-taree'; **is it a long way to ...?** haya
masēfa too-weela lil ...?; **would you
show me the way to do it?** mumkin
tewareenee izzay?; **do it this way**
a*amiloo kedda; **no way!** abadan!

we eHna; *see page 106*
weak (*person*) dIf; (*drink*) khafeef
wealthy ghenee
weather gow; **what foul weather!** e-
gow fazee-a*!; **what beautiful weather!** e-gow gameel!
weather forecast nashra gawaya
wedding Haflit gawaz
wedding anniversary *Iyeed e-zawag
e-sanawee
wedding ring khētim e-gawaz; (*in
Egypt also*) dibla
Wednesday yum el arba*
week isboo-a*; **a week (from) Sunday**
yum el Had e-gay; **Monday week**
yum litneen e-gay
weekend raHa isboo*Iya; **at/on the
weekend** yum e-gom*a
weight wazn; **I want to lose weight**
ana *a-Iyiz akhis shwIya
weight limit (*for baggage*) wazn
magēnee; (*for bridge*) wazn masmooH
weird (*person, custom, thing to happen*)
ghereeb
welcome: welcome to ... marHabban
lil ...; **you're welcome** (*don't mention
it*) *afwan
well: I don't feel well ana ta*ban
shwIya; **I haven't been very well**
ana kunt ta*ban shwIya; **she's not
well** haya ta*banna shwIya; **how are
you?** — **very well, thanks** (*said to
man*) izzayak? — kwIyis; (*said to
woman*) izzayik? — kwIyissa; **you
speak English very well** inta
bititkallim ingileezee kwIyis awee;
me as well ana kamen; **well done!**
mabrook!; **well well!** (*suprise*) halla
halla!
well-done (*meat*) mistoo-waya awee
Welsh ingileezee min 'wales'
were *see page 113*
west gharb; **to the west** lil gharb
Western afrangee
West Indian (*man, woman, adjective*)
min guzur el hind el gharbaya
West Indies guzur el hind el
gharbaya
wet mablool; **it's all wet** kuloo

mablool
wet suit (*for diving etc*) badlit ghats
what? ay?; **what's that?** edda?; **what
is he saying?** hoowa bee'ool ay?; **I
don't know what to do** ana mush
*arif a*mil ay; **what a view!** manzar
gameel!
wheel *agala
wheelchair korsee lil *agaza
when? emta?; **when does the bus
come?** emta el ōtōbees gay?, el
ōtōbees gay emta?; **when we get
back** lamma nerga*; **when we got
back** lamma riga*na
where? fayn?; **where is ...?** fayn ...?;
I don't know where he is ana mush
*arif hoowa fayn; **that's where I left
it** (*pointing*) ana sibtoo hena
which aya; (*with numbered items*) kam;
which street? aya shari*a?; **which
hotel?** aya fondō'?; **which one?** aya
waaHid?; **which bus number?**
ōtōbees kam?; **which flight number?**
reHla kam?; **which is yours?** fayn
bita*k?; **I forget which it was** mush
fēkhir aya waaHid; **the one which ...**
el waaHid ellee ...
while (*conjunction*) wa; **while I'm here**
wana hena
whisky 'whisky'
whisper (*verb*) washwish
white abeeyad
white wine nebeet abeeyad
who? meen?; **who was that?** meen
da?; **the man who ...** e-raagil ellee
...
whole: the whole week el isboo-a*
kuloo; **two whole days** yumayn
kamleen; **the whole lot** kuloohum
whooping cough e-so*īl e-deekee
whose: whose is this? da bita* meen?
why? lay?; **why not?** lay la'?, la' lay?;
that's why it's not working da e-
sabuhb ennoo mush shaghēl
wide *areed
wide-angle lens *adessa bizawee-a
kebeera
widow armalla
widower armuhl

wife zōga; **my wife** miraatee; **your
wife** miraatak
wig barooka
will: will you ask him? mumkin
tis'alloo?; *see page 110*
win (*verb*) kisib; **who won?** meen
kisib?
wind (*noun*) reeн (*f*)
window shebek; **near the window**
gamb e-shebek; **in the window** (*of
shop*) fil batreena
window seat korsee gamb e-shebek
windscreen, windshield barabreez
amāmee
**windscreen wipers, windshield
wipers** massaнat
windsurf: I'd like to windsurf ana
*a-ιyiz 'windsurf'
windsurfing 'windsurfing'
windy howa shedeed; **it's so windy**
e-reeн shedeeda awee
wine nebeet; **can we have some more
wine?** mumkin nebeet tanee?
wine glass kas nebeet
wine list kιmit e-nebeet
wing (*of plane, bird*) ginaн; (*of car*)
ruhfruhf
wing mirror mirraya
winter shitta; **in the winter** fi shitta
winter holiday agēzza shitwaya
wire silk
wireless radyō
wiring silk el kaharaba
wish: best wishes aateeyuhb el
amānee
with ma*; **with me** ma*aya; **with you**
ma*ak; **I'm staying with ...** ana ē-ιd
ma* ...; **with milk** bee laban
without min gheer
witness shēhid; **will you be a witness
for me?** mumkin teshadlee?
witty zareef
wobble: it wobbles (*wheel*) mush
mowzoona
woman sit
women sittāt
wonderful (*holiday, meal, weather,
person*) modhish
won't: it won't start mabidorsh; *see*

page 110

wood (*material*) khashab

wool soof

word kelma; **you have my word** (*I promise*) awiduhk

work (*verb*) ishtaghel; (*noun*) shoghl; **how does it work?** bitishtaghel izzay?; **it's not working** mush shaghel; **I work in an office** ana bashtaghel fee maktab; **do you have any work for me?** *andak shoghl laya?; **when do you finish work?** bitkhaalas shoghl emta?

world e-donya; **all over the world** fil *aluhm

worm (*parasitic*) dooda

worn-out (*person*) te*ib; (*shoes, clothes*) helkāna

worry: I'm worried about her ana el'ān *alayha; **don't worry** mate'la'sh

worry beads sebHa

worse: it's worse da aswuh'; **it's getting worse** da aswuh' min el owil

worst el aswuh'

worth: it's not worth 5 pounds da mi-istaHa'ish khamsa ginay; **it's worth more than that** da yistaHa' aktuhr min kedda; **is it worth a visit?** da yistaHa' e-zeeyara?

would: would you please ...? mumkin ...?; **would you give this to**

...? mumkin teddee da lee ...?; **what would you do?** Hata*mil ay?

wrap: could you wrap it up? mumkin telefoo?

wrapping laf

wrapping paper wara' lil laf

wrench (*tool*) muftaH ingileezee

wrist 'wrist'

write katab; **could you write it down?** mumkin tiktiboo?; **how do you write it?** tiktiboo izzay?; **I'll write to you** Haktiblak; **I wrote to you last month** ana katabtillak e-shahr elleefat

write-off: it's a write-off (*car etc*) matsaweesh Haga

writer kātib

writing kitāba; **Arabic writing** kitāba *arabaya

writing paper wara' lil kitāba

wrong: you're wrong inta ghaltaan; **the bill's wrong** el fatoora ghalat; **sorry, wrong number** asif, el nimra ghalat; **I'm on the wrong train** ana rikibt ghalat; **I went to the wrong room** ana roHt lee ōda tania; **that's the wrong key** mush da el muftaH; **there's something wrong with ...** fee *iyib fee ...; **what's wrong?** fee ay?; **what's wrong with it?** maloo?; **what's wrong with you?** malak?

X

X-ray esha*it 'X'

Y

yacht yakht
yacht club nēdee el yakht
yard: in the yard fil Hōsh; *see page 117*
year sana
yellow asfar
yellow fever Homa safra
yellow pages daleel telefōnet toogāree
Yemen: North Yemen el yemen e-shamalaya; South Yemen el yemen el ganoobaya
Yemeni (*man, adjective*) yamenee; (*woman*) yamanaya
yes ıwa
yesterday imbarraH; yesterday morning imbarraH e-subH; yesterday afternoon imbarraH e-dohr; the day before yesterday owel imbarraH
yet: has it arrived yet? wasuhl wala lessa?; not yet lessa

yobbo: he's a yobbo hoowa mushēghib
yog(h)urt zabādee
you (*to a man*) inta; (*to woman*) intee; (*plural*) intoo; this is for you da *alashēnak; with you ma*ak; *see page 106*
young sheb
young people shebeb
your: your house (*if owner male*) baytak; (*if owner female*) baytik; (*if referring to several people*) baytkoo; *see page 105*
yours (*if owner male*) da bita*ak; (*if owner female*) da bita*ik; (*if referring to several people*) da bita*akoo; *see page 108*
youth hostel bayt shebab; we're youth hostel(l)ing eHna beeno*d fee bayoot shebab
Yugoslavia yughoslavia

Z

zero sifr
zip, zipper sosta; could you put a new zip on? mumkin terakib sosta
gedeeda?
zoo gooninit el Hıawanet
zoom lens *adessa 'zoom'

Arabic – English

The signs and notices that you encounter will be in formal, Classical Arabic, which is essentially a written language, rarely spoken and quite distinct from colloquial Egyptian Arabic. Do not be surprised, therefore, to find that the pronunciation reveals differences between items as they occur in the English-Arabic and the Arabic-English sections of this book. Notice also that Arabic script runs from right to left.

LIST OF SUBJECT AREAS

Abbreviations
Airport and plane
Banks
Bars
Buses
Bus station
Cinemas, movie theaters
Clothing labels
Countries and nationalities
Cultural and historical interest
Customs
Days of the week
Department store sections
Doctors
Do not …
Drinks on menus
Eating and drinking places
Emergencies
Exclamations and swearwords
Food
Food labels
Forms
Garages
Geographical
Greetings
Hairdressers
Hospitals
Hotels
Medical

Medicine labels
Men's names
Months of the year
Movie theaters
Musicians, singers
Night spots
Notices in restaurants, bars, and on menus
Notices in shops
Notices on doors and gates
Place names
Post office
Public buildings
Public holidays (Egyptian)
Railway station
Replies
Restaurants
Rest rooms
Road signs
Schedules
Shop names
Streets
Taxis
Telephones
Theatres, theaters
Timetables, schedules
Toilets, rest rooms
Tourism
Youth hostel

ABBREVIATIONS

سم centimetres, centimeters

جم gram(me)s

س hours

كجم kilogram(me)s

كم kilometres, kilometers

لتر litres, liters

م metres, meters

مجم milligram(me)s

سم٣ millilitres, milliliters

مليم millimes

مم millimetres, millimeters

ق minutes

☙ piastres (*100 piastres = 1 Egyptian pound*)

☙ pounds (*Egyptian*)

B.C.C. Bank of Credit and Commerce

E.A.B. Egyptian American Bank

E.G.B. Egyptian Gulf Bank

I.C.I. International Language Centre/Center

I.L.I. International Language Institute

M.D.C. Masr (Egyptian) Development Company

N.E.C. Tele-masr Company, television and radio maufacture

J.V.C. Video Service Centre/Center

AIRPORT AND PLANE

وصول *[wisool]* arrivals

صالة الوصول *[saalit el wisool]* arrivals hall

بطاقة صعود *[bita'it so*ood]* boarding pass

النقد الأجنبي *[e-nuhkd el agnabee]* currency declaration office

صالة السفر *[saalit e-suhfuhr]* departure lounge

سوق حرة *[soo' Hora]* duty-free

للمصرين فقط *[lil masrayeen fakuht]* Egyptians only

رقم الرحلة *[rakuhm e-reHla]* flight number

للأجانب فقط *[lil agēnib fakuht]* foreigners only

استعلامات *[ista*lamat]* information

المفقودات *[el mafkoodet]* lost property, lost and found

رسائل *[rasē'il]* meeting point

ممنوع الدخول *[mamnoo-a* e-dikhool]* no entry

جوازات *[gawazēt]* passport control

خاص *[khaass]* private

العلاقات العامة *[el *ılakaat el *ama]* public relations office

دورات المياه *[dawaraat el meeyē]*

toilets, rest rooms

مرحباً [marHabban] welcome

BANKS

بنك إسكندرية [bank iskindraya]
Bank of Alexandria

بنك القاهرة [bank el kaheera] Cairo
Bank

الخزينة [el khazeena] cashier

حسابات جارية [Hisabāt gareeya]
current account, checking account

قسم العملة الأجنبية [kism el
*omla el agnabaya] foreign
exchange

الكارت الذهبي [el kart e-zahibee]
golden card, an Egyptian bank
card

بنك مصر [bank masr] Misr Bank

البنك الأهلي المصري [el bank el
ahlee el masree] National Bank of
Egypt

قرش [kuhrsh; spoken: uhrsh]
piastre (100 piastres = 1 Egyptian
pound)

☙ piastres (abbreviation)

جنيه [ginay] pounds (Egyptian)

☙ pounds (abbreviation for
Egyptian pounds)

حسابات التوفير [Hisabāt
e-towfeer] savings

سحب [saHb] withdrawals

BARS see **DRINKS** and **NOTICES
IN RESTAURANTS, BARS**

BUSES

ممنوع التدخين [mamnoo-a*
e-tadkheen] no smoking

مخصص لكبار السن فقط
[mokhassuhs li kubaar e-sin]
reserved for the elderly

التدخين مخالف للقانون
[e-tadkheen mokhellif lil kaanoon]
smoking is against the law

BUS STATION

رصيف . . . [raseef ...] bay
no. ..., lane no. ...

محطة أتوبيس [maHattit ōtōbees] bus
stop

هيئة النقل العام [hi'it e-na'l
el *am] General Transport
Company

CINEMAS, MOVIE THEATERS

حجز تذاكر [Hagz tazēkir] advance
bookings

بلكون [balakōn] balcony

شباك التذاكر [shebek e-tazēkir]
box office

الرجا مراجعة التذاكر والنقود قبل
مغادرة الشباك [e-raga morag*It
e-tazēkir wa e-nikood abl
moghadrit e-shebek] check your

tickets and change before
leaving the box office

سينما ['cinema'] cinema, movie
theater

ممنوع الخروج الا بعد انتهاء
الفيلم [mamnoo-a* el khuroog illa
ba*d intiha' el film] don't leave
before the performance ends

خروج [khuroog] exit

فوتيه لوج [losH] lounge

العرض القادم [el *ard el kaadim]
next show

ممنوع دخول المأكولات داخل
السينما [mamnoo-a* dikhool el
ma'koolet dekhil e-'cinema'] you
are not allowed to bring your own
food into the cinema/movie
theater

ممنوع التدخين داخل صالة العرض
[mamnoo-a* e-tadkheen
dekhil saalit el *ard] no smoking in
the auditorium

مواعيد الحفلات [mowa*Id el
Hafalet] performance times

حالياً [Halayan] showing now

صالة [saala] stalls

دورات المياه [dawaraat el meeyē]
toilets, rest rooms

CLOTHING LABELS

٤ age 4 years

صناعة مصرية [sina*a masraya]
Egyptian made

صنع في مصر [suna* fee masr]
made in Egypt

٤٤ size 44 (*British size 12*)

**COUNTRIES AND
NATIONALITIES**

الجزائر [el gazē-ir] Algeria

جزائرى [gaze-eeree] Algerian

أمريكا [amreeka] America

أمريكي [amreekee] American

البحرين [el baHrayn] Bahrain

مصر [masr] Egypt

مصري [masree] Egyptian

إنجلترا [ingilterra] England

إنجليزي [ingileezee] English

العراق [el *Irak; spoken: el *Ira']
Iraq

عراقي [*Irakee; spoken: *Ira'ee]
Iraqi

إسرائيل [isra-eel] Israel

إسرائيلي [isra-eelee] Israeli

الأردن [el ordun] Jordan

أردني [ordonnee] Jordanian

الكويت [koowayt] Kuwait

كويتي [koowaytee] Kuwaiti

لبناني [libnānee] Lebanese

لبنان [libnān] Lebanon

ليبيا [libya] Libya

ليبي *[leebee]* Libyan

مغربي *[maghribee]* Moroccan

المغرب *[el maghrib]* Morocco

عمان *[*aman]* Oman

فلسطين *[falastseen]* Palestine

فلسطيني *[falasteenee]* Palestinian

قطر *[kuhtuhr; spoken: uhtuhr]* Qatar

سعودي *[sa*oodee]* Saudi

السعودية *[e-so*daya]* Saudi Arabia

السودان *[e-soodan]* Sudan

سوداني *[soodanee]* Sudanese

سوريا *[suree-a]* Syria

سوري *[sooree]* Syrian

تونس *[toonis]* Tunisia

تونس *[toonissee]* Tunisian

تركيا *[torkaya]* Turkey

اليمن الشمالية *[el yamen e-shamalaya]* North Yemen

اليمن الجنوبية *[el yamen e-ganoobaya]* South Yemen

يمني *[yamenee]* Yemeni

CULTURAL AND HISTORICAL INTEREST

Islamic/religious

الله *[allah]* Allah

رب اجعل هذا بلداً آمناً *[rab eg*al haza baladan aminan]* Allah make this a safe country

الله أكبر *[allah akbar; spoken: allah wa akbar]* Allah is almighty

قبْلة *[ibla]* direction of Mecca

بسم الله الرحمن الرحيم *[bismillah e-raHman e-raHeem]* in the name of God most merciful

جمعية الإخوان المسلمين *[gam*Iyit el ekhwan el muslimeen]* The Islamic Brotherhood

القرآن *[el kur'aan]* Koran

محمد *[moHamed]* Mohamed

الصبر جميل *[e-sabr gameel]* patience is beautiful

رمضان *[ramadaan]* Ramadan

لا إله إلا الله *[la illah illa allah]* there is no other God but Allah

Political, people

أنور السادات *[anwar e-sadat]* Anwar Sadat, former President of Egypt

جمال عبد الناصر *[gamāl *abd e-nassir]* Gamal Abdel Nasser

الرئيس حسني مبارك *[e-ra'ees Hosnee moobaaruhk]* President Hosny Mubarak

الحزب الوطني الديمقراطي *[el Hezb el wotuhnee e-deemokraatee]* The National Democratic Party

Places, buildings

السد العالى *[e-sadd el *alee]* Aswan Dam

الجامع الأزرق [el gāmi*a el azra']
The Blue Mosque

برج القاهرة [borg el kaheera] Cairo
Tower

جامعة القاهرة [gama*it el kaheera]
Cairo University

حديقة الحيوانات [Hadeekit el
Hiawaanet] Cairo Zoo

المماليك [el mamaleek] City of the
Dead (Tombs of the Mamelukes)

مسجد الحسين [mazgid el Hossayn]
Hussein Mosque

جامع ابن طولون [gāmi*a ibn
tooloon] Ibn Tulun Mosque

المتحف الإسلامي [el matHaf el
islāmee] Islamic Museum

جامع الأزهر [mazgid el uhz-huhr]
el Uzar mosque

جامع محمد علي [gāmi*a moHamed
*alee] Mohamed Ali Mosque

جامع [gāmi*a] mosque

خان الخليلي [khan el khaleelee]
oriental bazaars

الموسكى [el muskee] street of the
oriental merchants

جامع السلطان حسن [gāmi*a
e-sultaan Hassan] Sultan Hassan
Mosque

الخليفة [el khaleefa] tombs of the
Caliphs

Ancient Egypt

كليوباترا [killee-obatra] Cleopatra

ايزيس [izees] Isis

نفرتارى ['nefertari'] Nefertari

نفرتيتى ['nefertiti'] Nefertiti

الأهرام [el ahraam] The Pyramids

رمسيس [ramsees] Ramses

أبو الهول [aboo el hol] The Sphinx

معبد أبو سمبل [ma*abad aboo
simbil] Temple of Abu Simbel

وادى الملوك [wēdee el milook]
Valley of the Kings

CUSTOMS

جمارك [gamarik] customs

للأجانب فقط [lil agēnib fakuht]
foreigners only

فى حدود المسموح [fee Hedood el
masmooH] nothing to declare

جوازات [gawazēt] passports

زيادة عن المسموح [zeeyada *an el
masmooH] something to declare

DAYS OF THE WEEK

السبت [yum e-sābt] Saturday

الأحد [yum el Had] Sunday

الأثنين [yum el itneen] Monday

الثلاثاء [yum e-talaat] Tuesday

الأربعاء [yum el arba*a] Wednesday

الخميس [yum el khamees] Thursday

الجمعة [yum e-gom*a] Friday

أيام [Iyēm] days

DEPARTMENT STORE SECTIONS

بياضات [bIyadaat] bed linen

سجاد وموكيت [sigad wa mukitt] carpets

قسم الشباب [kism e-shebab] casual clothes

قسم الأطفال [kism el atfaal] childrens' department

ساعات وفضيات [sa*at wa fedeeyaat] clocks, watches and silver

أدوات تجميل [adawet tagmeel] cosmetics

أقطان [aktaan] cottons (fabric)

موبيليا [mobilya] furniture

روائح وهدايا [rawIyaH wa hadaya] gifts and perfumes

أدوات منزلية [adawet manzilaya] hardware

مجوهرات [moogow-haraat] jewel(le)ry

جاهز سيدات [gehiz sayeedat] ladies' fashions

لانجيري [langeeree] lightweight fabrics

ملابس داخلية للسيدات [malabis dakhilaya lil sayeedat] lingerie

جاهز رجالي [gehiz rigālee] mens' fashions

أصواف رجالي [aswaaf rigālee] mens' tailoring fabrics in wool

راديو وتلفزيون [radyo wa televizyōn] radio and television

قمصان [umsaan] shirts

أحذية [aHzaya] shoes

حراير [Harrayuhr] silks

لعب أطفال [le*ab atfaal] toys and games

ديكور [dikor] wallpapers

DOCTORS see MEDICAL

DO NOT …

خطر [khattuhr] danger

خطر لا تلمس [khattuhr la talmis] dangerous, don't touch

ممنوع الجلوس على الخضرة [mamnoo-a* el giloos *ala el khodra] do not sit on the grass

لا تستعمل آلة التنبيه [la testa*mil elit e-tambee] do not sound your horn

ممنوع … [mamnoo-a* …] … forbidden

منطقة عسكرية
ممنوع الاقتراب والتصوير [muhntee'a *askaraya mamnoo-a* el ektirab wa e-tuhsweer] military zone, keep clear, no photography

ممنوع لعب الكرة *[mamnoo-a*
le*ab el kora]* no ball games

ممنوع الاستحمام *[mamnoo-a* el
estiHmem]* no bathing

ممنوع التخييم *[mamnoo-a*
e-takheem]* no camping

ممنوع الدخول *[mamnoo-a*
e-dikhool]* no entry

ممنوع الانتظار *[mamnoo-a* el
intizaar]* no parking

ممنوع التصوير *[mamnoo-a*
e-tuhsweer]* no photographs

ممنوع التدخين *[mamnoo-a*
e-tadkheen]* no smoking

ممنوع الوقوف *[mamnoo-a* el
wokoof]* no stopping

ممنوع السباحة *[mamnoo-a*
e-sibaHa]* no swimming

ممنوع المرور *[mamnoo-a* el muroor]*
no trespassing

DRINKS ON MENUS

سفن أب *['7 Up']* 7-Up (tm)

قهوة كابتشينو *[ahwa 'cappuccino']*
cappuccino coffee

خروب *[kharoob]* carob

كوكاكولا *[kakōla]* coca cola (tm)

كاكاو *[kakow]* cocoa

سبورت كولا *['sport cola']* diet coke
(tm)

قهوة أكسبرسو *[ahwa 'espresso']*
espresso coffee

عصير موز *[*aseer mooz]* fresh
banana milk shake

عصير جزر *[*aseer guhzuhr]* fresh
carrot juice

عصير جوافة *[*aseer guwafa]* fresh
guava juice

عصير ليمون *[*aseer lamoon]* fresh
lemonade

عصير برتقال *[*aseer bortookaan;
spoken: *aseer bortoo'aan]* fresh
orange juice

عصير فراولة *[*aseer farowla]*
strawberry juice

عصير قصب *[*aseer asuhb]* fresh
sugar cane juice

جرب فروت *[graybfroot]*
grapefruit juice

حلبة *[Helba]* helba, drink made
from boiled fenugreek seeds

كركدية *[karkadāy]* hibiscus drink

بيرة ستلا *[beera stella]* lager

عرقسوس *[*arkoosoos; spoken:
ar'oosoos] liquorice, licorice

عصير مانجو *[*aseer manga]* mango
juice

مياه معدنية *[meeyē ma*adanaya]*
mineral water

كوكتيل *['cocktail']* mixed fruit juices

كندا دراى ['canada dry'] mixers

تيم [teem (tm)] orange drink

بيبسى كولا ['pepsi'] pepsi (tm)

سحلب [saHlab] similar to Horlicks (tm)

صودا ['soda'] soda water

مشروب بيرل [mashroob birl] spa (spring) water

تمر هندي [tamr hindee] tamarind juice

شاى [shay] tea

قهوة [ahwa] Turkish coffee

EATING AND DRINKING PLACES

بار ['bar'] bar

بوفيه [buffay] café

نادى [nēdee] coffee and gaming house

كشرى [kōsharee] eat-in (or take-away) for 'kosharee', a typical Egyptian rice speciality

جروبى [grobbee] Groppi – the best ice cream parlour/parlor and patisserie in Cairo

عصير وفواكه [*aseer wa fawakih] juice bar

حاتى [Hattee] kebab house

فطاطرى [fataatree] pastry shop

حلوانى [Halawēnee] patisserie

كازينو ['casino'] picturesque tea room and bar, usually by the Nile

مطعم [mat*am] restaurant

كافيتريا ['cafeteria'] snack bar

فلفلة [filfilla] the best known restaurant for authentic Egyptian food

قهوة [ahwa] traditional coffee house

EMERGENCIES

الجمهورية [el gomhoraya] 24-hour pharmacy service

إسعاف [isa*af] ambulance

مطافى القاهرة [mataafee el kaheera] Cairo Fire Brigade/Department

مديرية أمن القاهرة [modarayit amn el kaheera] Cairo Police H.Q.

قسم الدقى [kism e-dokkee; spoken: e-do'ee] Dokki Police Station (opposite Sheraton Hotel, Cairo)

مخرج [makhruhg] emergency exit

حنفية حريق [Hanafayit Haree'] fire hydrant

قسم . . . [kism . . .] police station for … (name of area)

شرطة السكة الحديد [shortit e-sikka el Hadeed] Railway/Railroad Police

شرطة السياحة [shortit e-seeyēHa] Tourist Police

EXCLAMATIONS AND SWEARWORDS

allah wa akbar! *God almighty!*

ela*na! *damn!*

ghebee! *fool!, idiot!*

hala hala! *well, well!, well I never!*

Hasib! *look out!*

inta*ama? *are you blind?*

mush teHasib? *can't you watch what you're doing?*

ya salēm! *my goodness! (literally: oh peace!)*

FOOD

Oriental hors d'oeuvres, Starters and side dishes

بابا غنوج *[baba ghanoog]* aubergine/eggplant purée

فول مدمس *[fool midamis]* brown bean purée, Egyptian national dish

تبولة *[taboola]* cracked wheat and tomato salad

طعمية *[ta*amaya]* fried balls of ground beans and herbs

سلطة خضراء *[salata khadra]* green salad

بذنجان مخلل *[bitingan mikhallil]* marinated aubergine/eggplant

سلطة شرقى *[salata shar'ee]* oriental (mixed vegetable) salad

حمص *[Hommos]* puréed chickpeas

طحينة *[taHeena]* sesame seed paste

سلطة بيضة *[salata bayda]* spiced yoghurt served with herbs

ورق عنب *[warak *Inab; spoken: wara']* stuffed vine leaves

سلطة طماطم *[saltit tomaatim]* tomato salad

جبنة بيضاء بالطماطم *[gibna bayda bi tomaatim]* white cheese with tomato salad

Soups

شوربة فراخ *[shorbit ferēkh]* chicken soup

فتة *[fata]* feastday soup of meat stock from a sacrificial lamb, with bread, rice and tomato

شوربة عدس *[shorbit *ads]* lentil soup

شوربة لحمة *[shorbit laHma]* meat soup

ملوخية *[molokhaya]* traditional soup laden with garlic and made from a spinach-like Egyptian vegetable of the marrow family

شوربة خضار *[shorbit khodaar]* vegetable soup

Egg dishes

عجة *[*Iga]* baked omelet(te) with onion

بيض مسلوق *[bayd masloo']* boiled eggs

بيض مقلى *[bayd ma'allee]* fried eggs

أومليت *['omelette']* omelet(te)

بيض بكبدة فراخ *[bayd bi kibdit ferekh]* scrambled eggs with chopped chicken liver

بيض بسطرمة *[bayd basterma]* scrambled eggs with cold meat

شكشوكة *[shakshooka; spoken: sha'shoo'a]* scrambled eggs with mince/ground beef

Meat and meat dishes

مخ *[mokh]* brains

لحمة كندوز *[laHma kandooz]* braising meat

فراخ *[ferēkh]* chicken

بط *[buht]* duck

لحم فلتو *[laHm flittoo]* fillet mignon

وز *[wizz]* goose

مشويات متنوعة *[mashweeyēt]* grills

نصف فرخة مشوية *[nus ferkha mashwaya]* half a grilled chicken

شيش كباب وكفتة *[sheesh kebab wi kofta]* kebabs with meatballs

لحم ضانى بريانى *[laHm daanee 'biryani']* lamb biryani

كبدة *[kibda]* liver

لحمة بتلو *[laHma bi telloo]* meat on the bone

لحمة ضانى *[laHma daanee]* mutton

حمام *[Hammem]* pigeon

أرانب *[arānib]* rabbit

سجق *[soogo']* similar to haggis

شاورمة *[shawerma]* slices of spit-roast lamb

لحمة أوزى *[laHma oozee]* spring lamb

ريش لحم بقرى *[reesh laHm ba'ree]* steak on the bone

حمام محشى *[Hammem maHshee]* stuffed pigeon

ديك رومي *[deek roomee]* turkey

اسكالوب بتلو *['escaloppe' bi telloo]* veal escalope

Vegetarian dishes

كرنب محشى *[kuromb maHshee]* stuffed cabbage

كوسة محشية *[kosa maHshaya]* stuffed courgettes/zucchinis

فلفل محشى *[filfil maHshee]* stuffed peppers

بطاطس محشية *[bataatis maHshaya]* stuffed potatoes

طاجن خضار *[taagin khodaar]* vegetables baked with tomatoes

Rice, pulses, pasta

كشرى *[kōsharee]* a mixture of rice, lentils, macaroni and onions with a hot tomato sauce

لوبيا *[lobia]* beans (*small black-eyed*)

فول *[fool]* brown Egyptian beans

حمص [*Hommos*] chickpeas

فريك [*fireek*] cracked wheat

طعمية [*ta*amaya*] deep-fried balls of spiced bean purée

فاصوليا [*fasolia*] haricot beans

عدس بجبة [**ads (bigebba)*] lentils (*small brown*)

مكرونة [*makarōna*] macaroni

شعرية [*sha*raya*] noodles, vermicelli

عدس أصفر [**ads (asfar)*] orange lentils

فول مدمس [*fool midamis*] puréed brown Egyptian beans

رز [*ruz*] rice

رز بشعرية [*ruz bi sha*raya*] rice with noodles

مكرونة عيدان [*makarōna *ɪdan*] spaghetti

Fish and fish dishes

طاجن سمك [*taagin samak*] baked fish

قراميط [*arameet*] catfish

كابوريا [*kaboree-a*] crab

تعابين [*ta*abeen*] eels

ترنشات [*taranshaat*] fillets

. . . مقلى [*... ma'allee*] fried ...

. . . مشوى [*... mashwee*] grilled ...

. . . بزيت [*... bi zayt*] ... in oil

بورى [*booree*] mullet

طاجن جمبرى [*taagin gambaree*] potted shrimps

جمبرى [*gambaree*] prawns

أرز بالجمبرى [*ruz bi gambaree*] prawns and rice

رنجة [*ringuh*] salted fish

سردين [*'sardine'*] sardines

مكرونة [*makarōna*] type of fish

بلطى [*boltee*] type of freshwater fish

مرجان [*morgan*] type of freshwater fish

Types of bread

عيش [**ɪ-esh*] bread

فينو [*feeno medowar*] bread rolls

عيش بلدى [**ɪ-esh baladee*] round, flat, rough wholemeal

عيش شامى [**ɪ-esh shāmee*] round, flat, white pitta-type bread

سندوتش [*'sandwich'*] sandwich

سميط [*simeet*] sesame-crusted bread rings

فينو [*feenō*] whitish baguette (*French loaf*)

Vegetables

خرشوف [*kharshoof*] artichokes

بتنجان [*bitingan*] aubergines, eggplants

فول حيراتي [fool Heraatee] broad beans

كرنب [kuromb] cabbage

جزر [guhzuhr] carrots

قرنبيط [arnabeet] cauliflower

فلفل حامي [filfil Hāmee] chillies

كوسة [kosa] courgettes, zucchinis

آته [ata] cucumber (large)

خيار [kheeyar] cucumber (small)

توم [tom] garlic

فاصوليا [fasolia] green beans

فلفل أخضر [filfil akhdar] green peppers

خس [khass] lettuce

نعناع [ne*ana*] mint

بامية [bamya] okra, ladies' fingers

بصل [basal] onions

بقدونس [ba'doonis] parsley

بسلة [bisilluh] peas

بطاطس [bataatis] potatoes

سبانخ [sabenekh] spinach, beet

بصل أخضر [basal akhdar] spring onions

ذوره [dora] sweet corn, maize

بطاطا [bataataa] sweet potatoes

طماطم [oota] tomatoes

لفت [lift] turnips

ورق عنب [wara' *Inab] vine leaves

جرجير [guhrgir] watercress

فجل [figl] white radish

Fruit and nuts

لوز [loz] almonds

تفاح [tufē-aH] apples

مشمش [mishmish] apricots

موز [mooz] bananas

جوز الهند [gooz el hind] coconut

بلح [balaH] dates

تين [teen] figs

عنب [*Inab] grapes (large, sweet and yellow)

عنب بناتي [*Inab banatee] grapes (small and seedless)

جوافة [gawafa] guava

بندق [bundo'] hazelnuts

ليمون أصفر [lamoon (asfar)] lemons

ليمون [lamoon] limes

مانجة [manga] mango

شمام [shamēm] melon

توت [toot] mulberries

برتقال بسرة [bortoo'aan bisora] oranges (of the large navel kind)

خوخ [khokh] peaches

فول سوداني [fool sudanee] peanuts

كمثرى [komitruh] pears

حمص [Hommos] peas (small and roasted)

أناناس *[ananas]* pineapple

فستق *[fozdo']* pistachio nuts

رومان *[romaan]* pomegranates

لب *[lib]* roasted seeds (*of melon, sunflower etc*)

يوسفى *[ostafendee]* satsumas

فراولة *[farowla]* strawberries

عين جمل *[*in gamal]* walnuts

بطيخ *[bateekh]* water melon

برقوق *[barkook; spoken: bar'oo']* plums

برتقال *[bortookaan; spoken: bortoo'aan]* oranges

Cakes, sweets and desserts

جلاش *[gulesh]* baklava – fine layers of pastry and nuts soaked in syrup

بسبوسة *[basboosa]* cake made with semolina and soaked in syrup

خشاف *[khoshēf]* compote of stewed fruits eaten during Ramadan

زلابية *[zalabiya]* fritters soaked in syrup

فروت سلاط *['fruit salad']* fruit salad

مهلبية *[mahalabaya]* ground rice with milk and rosewater

آيس كريم *['ice cream']* ice cream

بلوظة *[balooza]* milk pudding made with cornflour

قطايف *[attf]* pancake, thick and stuffed with nuts

أرز باللبن *[ruz bi laban]* rice pudding

كنافة *[kunafa]* sticky pastry with nuts and syrup

أم على *[um *alee]* traditional pudding made with raisins, cake and milk

Basics

بسكويت *[baskaweet]* biscuits, cookies

زبدة *[zebda]* butter

جبنة *[gibna]* cheese

سمنة *[samna]* clarified butter

قهوة *[ahwa]* coffee

بيض *[bayd]* eggs

دقيق *[di'ee']* flour

عسل نحل *[*asal naHl]* honey

مربة *[mirabuh]* jam

لبن *[laban]* milk

عسل اسود *[*asal eswid]* molasses

زيت *[zayt]* oil

زيت زيتون *[zayt zetoon]* olive oil

فلفل أسود *[filfil eswid]* pepper

ملح *[malH]* salt

سكر *[sukar]* sugar

شاى [shay] tea

خل [khel] vinegar

زبادى [zabēdee] yoghurt

Cheeses

جبنة رومى [gibna roomee] hard cheese

جبنة نستو [gibna nistoo] processed cheese wedges

جبنة بيضة [gibna bayda] salty white cheese

جبنة فلاحى [gibna fellaнee] similar to cottage cheese

جبنة قديمة [gibna adeema] strongly matured 'gibna fellaнee'

جبنة تلاجة [gibna talēga] very mild white cheese

FOOD LABELS

المحتويات [el moнtawayēt] contents

تاريخ الانتاج [tareekh el intag] date of manufacture

الوزن الصافى [el wazn e-saafee] net weight

السعر للمستهلك [e-se*ar lil mustahlik] price

بروتينات [brōteenēt] protein

تاريخ الانتهاء [tareekh el intiha'] sell-by date

سكريات [sukareeyēt] sugar

مدة الصلاحية [modit e-salaнaya ...] will keep for ...

قيتامينات [vitameenēt] vitamins

FORMS

العنوان address

العنوان فى مصر address in Egypt

التاريخ date

تاريخ الميلاد date of birth

تاريخ الإصدار date of issue

مدة الاقامة duration of stay

الاسم بالكامل full name

الجنسية nationality

المهنة occupation

رقم جواز السفر passport number

جهة الميلاد place of birth

جهة الإصدار place of issue

الديانة religion

توقيع signature

رقم التأشيرة visa number

GARAGES

هواء [howa] air

خدمة الغسيل الآلى [khedmit el gheseel el alee] automatic car wash

موقف سيارات [mow'af siyaraat] car park, parking lot

فرش ودواسات السيارات [farsh wa dawāset e-siyaraat] car upholstery sales

الدخول ببطء [e-dikhool bee bot'] enter slowly

بيع وأصلاح اطارات *[be*a wa islaaH etaaraat]* full tyre/tire service

هدايا ولعب أطفال *[hadaya wa le*ab atfaal]* gifts and children's games

الخروج ببطء *[el khuroog bee bot']* leave slowly

تشحيم وتغيير زيت *[tashHeem wi tagheer zayt]* lubrication and oil change

موبيل *[mobil]* mobil (*tm*)

ممنوع التدخين *[mamnoo-a* e-tadkheen]* no smoking

غسيل راديتير *[gheseel 'radiator']* radiator water change

بنزين مخصوص *[benzeen makhsoos]* special grade petrol/gas

بنزين سوبر ٨٠ *[benzeen 'super 80']* super 80 petrol/gas

بنزين سوبر ٩٠ *[benzeen 'super 90']* super 90 petrol/gas

اطارات وبطاريات *[etaaraat wa battareeyaat]* tyres/tires and batteries

جراج *['garage']* underground parking

ضبط زوايا واتزان *[duhbt zawaya wa etizan]* wheel balancing

GEOGRAPHICAL

حدود *[Hedood]* border

قناة *[koneh]* canal

دلتا *[deltuh]* delta

صحراء *[saHra]* desert

مركز *[markaz]* district

شرق *[shar']* east

محافظة *[moHafzuh]* governorate, administrative district

خليج *[khaleeg]* gulf

جزيرة *[gezeeruh]* island

بركة *[birka]* lake

جبل *[gabal]* mount

شمال *[shimēl]* north

واحة *[weHa]* oasis

راس *[ras]* point, head

مديرية *[modoraya]* province

نهر *[nahr]* river

ملاحة *[malēHa]* salt lake

جنوب *[ganoob]* south

عين *[*In]* spring

وادى *[wēdee]* valley

غرب *[gharb]* west

GREETINGS *see* **REPLIES**

HAIRDRESSERS

كوافير . . . *[kowafayar]* ladies' hairdresser

صالون . . . *[salōn ...]* ... salon

HOSPITALS *see* **MEDICAL**

HOTELS

بنسيون [benseeyōn] boarding house

الخزينة [el khazeena] cashier

فندق [fondō'] hotel

الاستعلامات [el ista*lamat] information

الاستقبال [el isti'bel] reception

لوكاندة [lokanduh] small hotel

دورة المياه [dowrit el meeyē] toilet, rest room

MEDICAL

قسم استقبال الحوادث [kism isti'bel el Howādis] casualty department

عيادة [*Iyāda] clinic

جراح أسنان [garaH asnan] dentist

اخصائي أمراض جلدية [akhissaa'ee uhmraad gildaya] dermatologist

دكتور . . . [doktor ...] Dr ...

جراح أنف وأذن وحنجرة [garaH ozuhn wa anf wa Hungara] ear, nose and throat specialist

جراح عيون [garaH *Iyoon] eye specialist

أخصائي أمراض القلب [akhissaa'ee uhmraad el alb] heart specialist

مستشفى [mustashfa] hospital

أخصائي ولادة وأمراض نساء [akhissaa'ee wilāda wa uhmraad nissa] obstetrician and gyn(a)ecologist

أخصائي بصريات [akhissaa'ee basareeyaat] optician

جراح عظام [garaH *Izaam] orthop(a)edic doctor

أخصائي عظام [akhissaa'ee *Izaam] orthop(a)edic specialist

قسم العيادة الخارجية [kism el *Iyēda el kherigaya] out-patients

MEDICINE LABELS

للبالغين adults

حقن ampoules

حسب ارشادات الطبيب as directed by the physician

متوسط الجرعة اليومية average daily dose

كبسولات capsules

للأطفال الكبار children

التركيب composition

الجرعة dose/dosage

الأثر الطبى indications

للأطفال الرضع infants

مجم mg

سم٣ ml

قرص ٣ مرات يوميا one tablet three times daily

ملعقة صغيرة كل ٤ أو ٦ ساعات
يومياً one teaspoonful every
4-6 hours

الأثار الجانبية side effects

معلق suspension

أقراص tablets

ملعقة صغيرة teaspoonful

MEN'S NAMES

عبد الـ . . . Abdel ...

أبو Abu

عادل Adel

أحمد Ahmed

على Ali

أشرف Ashraf

عاصم Assam

عاطف Atef

جمال Gamal

حسن Hassan

حسين Hussein

إبراهيم Ibrahim

خالد Khaled

محمود Mahmood

منصور Mansoor

محمد Mohamed

محسن Mohsen

مختار Mokhtar

مصطفى Mustapha

نبيل Nabil

ناصر Nasser

عمر Omar

صلاح Salah

صالح Saleh

سمير Samir

سيد Sayeed

طاهر Taher

MONTHS OF THE YEAR

يناير *[yanaayuhr]* January

فبراير *[fibrıuhr]* February

مارس *[mēris]* March

أبريل *[abreel]* April

مايو *[mayoo]* May

يونيو *[yoonyoo; spoken: yoonya]*
June

يوليو *[yulyoo; spoken: yulya]* July

أغسطس *[aghostos]* August

سبتمبر *[sibtimbuhr]* September

أكتوبر *[oktōbuhr]* October

نوفمبر *[novimbuhr]* November

ديسمبر *[disimbuhr]* December

شهور *[shuhor]* months

MOVIE THEATERS *see* **CINEMAS**

MUSICIANS, SINGERS

عبد الحليم Abdel Haleem

عبد الوهاب Abdel Wahebb

فريد الأطرش Fareed el Atruhsh

فيروز Fayrooz

أم كلثوم Um Khalsoom

وردة Warda

NIGHT SPOTS

بار ['bar'] bar

كازينو ['casino'] bar in romantic spot along the Nile

كابريه ['cabaret'] cabaret

ملهى ليلى [malha laylee] night club

صحارى سيتى ['sahara city'] night club in a tent in the desert outside Cairo with the most varied floorshow of traditional dancing

NOTICES IN RESTAURANTS, BARS AND ON MENUS

٪١٠ خدمة [10% khedma] 10% service charge

مشروبات [mashroobaat] drinks

أطباق البيض [uhtbaa'el bayd] egg dishes

مشويات [mashweeyēt] grills

أطباق شرقية [uhtbaa' shar'aya] oriental dishes

نشويات [nashweeyēt] rice and pastas

أنواع الشرب [anwa* e-shoruhb] soups

حلويات [Halaweeyēt] sweets, desserts

الأسعار شاملة الخدمة والضريبة [el as*ar shamla el khedma wa e-dareeba] taxes and services included

الادارة ترحب بكم دائماً [el idaara tooraHib bikum dayimman] the management welcomes you

دورة المياه [dowrit el meeyē] toilet, rest room

NOTICES IN SHOPS

خزينة [khazeena] cashier

كنترول ['control'] goods collection point

البضاعة المباعة لا ترد ولا تستبدل [el beda*a el mobe*a la tooruhd walla tustabdel] no exchange or refund

أسعارنا في متناول الجميع [as*aruhnna fee mutanawil e-gamee*a] our prices are modest

مدير الفرع [modeer el farra*] store manager

الزبون دائماً على حق [e-ziboon dayimman *ala Hak] the customer is always right

دورة المياه [dowrite el meeyē] toilet, rest room

شيكات سياحية للبيع هنا [sheekat seeyaHaya lil bay*a hena] traveller's cheques/traveler's checks sold here

NOTICES ON DOORS AND GATES

هواء مكيف *[howa' mookayif]*
air-conditioned

مغلق *[moghluhk]* closed

العطلة الأسبوعية *[el *otla el
isboo-*ɪya]* closing days

دخول *[dikhool]* entrance

خروج *[khuroog]* exit

من . . . إلى . . . *[min … illa …]*
from … to …

المدير *[el modeer]* manager's office

ممنوع الدخول *[mamnoo-a*
e-dikhool]* no entry

ممنوع الوقوف امام البوابة
[mamnoo-a el wookoof amam el
bewaba]* no parking in front of
these gates

مفتوح *[maftooH]* open

مواعيد العمل *[mowa*ɪd el *amal]*
opening hours

اسحب *[esHab]* pull

ادفع *[edfa*]* push

مرحبا *[marHabban]* welcome

PLACE NAMES

العباسية *[el *abbasaya]* Abbasiya

عابدين *[*abdeen]* Abdin

أبو سمبل *[aboo simbil]* Abu Simbel

العجوزة *[el *agooza]* Aguza

الاسكندرية *[el iskindraya]*
Alexandria

أسيوط *[assyoot]* Assyut

أسوان *[aswaan]* Aswan

ميدان العتبة *[midan el *ataba]*
Ataba Square

باب الخلق *[bab el khal']* Bab
el Khalq

باب اللوق *[babelook; spoken:
babeloo']* Bab el Ook

باب زويلة *[bab ziwayla]*
Bab Zuwaila

بنى سويف *[benee swayf]* Beni Suef

القاهرة *[el kaheera]* Cairo

القلعة *[el al*a]* Citadel

دهب *[dahab]* Dahab

دهشور *[dahshur]* Dashur

الدقى *[e-dokkee; spoken: e-do'ee]*
Dokki

إدفو *[edfoo]* Edfu

البدرشين *[el badrasheen]* El
Badrshein

الفيوم *[el fayoom]* El Faiyum

الخارجة *[el kharga]* El Kharga

المنصورة *[el mansoora]* El Mansura

المنيا *[el minya)* El Minya

الموسكى *[el muskee]* El Muski

السيدة زينب *[e-sayeda zaynab]*
El Saiyida Zeinab

إسنا *[esna]* Esna

جاردن سيتى *['garden city']*
Garden City

الجيزة *[el geezuh]* Giza

دير البحارى *[dē-ir el baнaree]*
Hatshepsut's temple

مصر الجديدة *[masr el gedeeda]*
Heliopolis

حلوان *[нelwān]* Helwan

إمبابة *[imbaba]* Imbaba

الاسماعيلية *[el isma*laya]* Ismailia

الكرنك *[el karnak]* Karnak

مرسى مطروح *[marsa matrooн]*
Marsa Matruh

المقطم *[el Mokattam; spoken:*
el mo'attam] Mokattam

مدينة نصر *[medeenit nasr]* Nasser
City

القرنة الجديدة *[el gurna e-gedeeda]*
New Gurna

مصر القديمة *[masr el adeema]*
Old Cairo

القرنة القديمة *[el gurna el adeema]*
Old Gurna

بورسعيد *[bor sa*yeed]* Port Said

قنا *[kenna; spoken: enna]* Kena

خان الخليلى *[khan el khaleelee]*
Khan el Khalili

كوم أمبو *[komumboo]* Kom Ombo

ميدان التحرير *[midan e-taнreer]*
Liberation Square

الأقصر *[el lu'sor]* Luxor

المعادى *[el ma*adee]* Maadi

المنيل *[el manyal]* Manial or Geziret
el Roda

ميدان رمسيس *[midan ramsees]*
Ramses Square

سقارة *[Sakkara; spoken: sa'ara]*
Sakkara

شرم الشيخ *[sharuhm e-shekh)*
Sharm el Sheikh

سينا *[seena]* Sinai

سيوة *[seewa]* Siwa

سوهاج *[soohag]* Sohag

السويس *[el Soo-is]* Suez

طنطا *[tuhntuh]* Tante

مدينة هابو *[medeenit haboo]*
temples of Ramses

وادى الملوك *[wēdee el milook]*
Valley of the Kings

وادى الملكات *[wēdee el maleekat]*
Valley of the Queens

وادى حوف *[wēdee Hof]*
Wadi Halfa

زمالك *[zamalik]* Zamalik

POST OFFICE

بريد جوى *[bareed gawee]* airmail

مستعجل *[mista*gil]* express

قابل للكسر *[kaabil lil kasr]* fragile

خطابات داخلية *[khitabaat dakhilaya]* inland mail

صندوق بريد *[sandoo' bareed]* letterbox

خطابات *[khitabaat]* letters

عادى *[*adee]* ordinary

عادى ١٠ جرام الدول العربية *[el *arabaya *adee e-diwil]* rate for 10g to other Arab countries

بيع الطوابع *[be*a e-tawaabe*a]* postage stamps

رسوم التخليص *[risoom e-taakhlees]* postal charges

مكتب بريد *[maktab bareed]* post office

عادى ١٠ جرام الدول الأجنبية *[*adee e-diwil el agnabaya]* rate for 10g to non-Arab countries

خطابات خارجية *[khitabaat kherigaya]* overseas mail

مستعجل ٢٠ جرام *[mista*gil]* rate for 20g express service

عادى ٢٠ جرام *[*adee]* rate for 20g inland mail

PUBLIC BUILDINGS

جامعة عين شمس *[gama*it *In shams]* Ain Shams University

المعهد البريطاني *[el ma*had el britaanee]* British Council

محافظة القاهرة *[moHuhfzit el kaheera]* Cairo Governorate HQ

متحف الآثار *[matHaf el asaar]* Cairo Museum of Antiquities

متحف البريد *[matHaf el bareed]* Cairo Postal Museum

القصر العينى *[el asr el *Ianee]* Cairo University Medical School

. . . قنصلية *[konsulayit ...]* Consulate of ...

. . . سفارة *[safaarit ...]* Embassy of ...

. . . كلية *[kullayit ...]* faculty of ...

المجمع *[el mogamma]* Government Central Department of Information (*Cairo*)

. . . مستشفى *[mustashfa ...]* ... Hospital

مكتبة *[maktaba]* library

. . . وزارة *[wizaarit ...]* Ministry of ...

وزارة الزراعة *[wizaarit e-zira*a]* Ministry of Agriculture

وزارة السياحة *[wizaarit e-seeyēHa]* Ministry of Tourism

. . . متحف *[matHaf ...]* museum of ...

مكتب تلغراف وتليفون *[maktab teleghraaf wa telefōn]* Office for Telegraphs and Telephones

. . . قسم *[kism ...]* ... Police

Station

مبنى الأذاعة والتلفزيون [mabna el iza*a wa e-televizyōn] Radio and Television Building (Cairo)

محطة . . . [maHattit ...] ... railway station, ... train station

مدرسة . . . [madrassit ...] ... school

PUBLIC HOLIDAYS (EGYPTIAN)

عيد تحرير سيناء [*Iyeed taHreer seena] Sinai Liberation Day (April 25th)

عيد العمال [*Iyeed el *omēl] Labour/Labor Day (May 1st)

عيد الثورة [*Iyeed e-sowra] Anniversary of the Revolution (July 23rd)

عيد القوات المسلحة ـ عيد ٦ أكتوبر [*Iyeed el koowat el musalaHa] Armed Forces Day (Oct 6th)

عيد النصر [*Iyeed e-nuhsr] Victory Day (Dec 23rd)

عيد الأضحى [*Iyeed el uhdHa; spoken: el *Iyeed e-kebeer] Big Feast

رأس السنة الهجرية [raas e-sana el hegraya] Islamic New Year

المولد النبوى الشريف [el mowlid e-nabowee e-shereef] Mohamed's birthday

عيد الفطر [*Iyeed el fitr; spoken: el *Iyeed e-sooghIyar] Small Feast

شم النسيم [sham e-nesseem] Spring Celebration

RAILWAY STATION

حجز تذاكر . . . [Hagz tazēkir ...] advance booking for ...

استراحة [istiraHa] buffet

محطة مصر [maHattit masr] Cairo Main Railway/Railroad Station

هيئة سكك حديد مصر [hI'it sikkuhk Hadeed masr] Egypt Railways/Railroad

درجة أولى . . . [... daraga oola] first class

اسعاف محطة القاهرة [is*af maHattit el kaheera] first aid post

معلومات [ma*loomēt] information

امانات [amanēt] left luggage, baggage checkroom

رصيف . . . [raseef ...] platform no. ..., track no. ...

درجة ثانية . . . [... daraga tania] second class

درجة ثالثة . . . [... daraga talta] third class

شباك تذاكر . . . [shebek tazēkir] ticket office

تذاكر [tazēkir] tickets

REPLIES

shukran *thank you*

*afwan *not at all, don't mention it*

el *afw *not at all, don't mention it*

sabaH el kheer *good morning*

sabaH e-noor *good morning* (*reply*)

misē' el kheer *good evening*

misē' e-noor *good evening* (*reply*)

salemmoo *aleekum *hello*

*aleekum e-salēm *hello* (*reply*)

izzayak? (*to man*); izzayik? (*to woman*) *how are you?*

kwɪyis (*said by man*); kwɪyissa (*said by woman*) *I'm fine*

el Hamdu lillah *I'm fine* (*literally – thanks be to God*)

wa inta? (*to man*); wa intee? (*to woman*) *and you?*

ahlan *welcome*

ahlan wa sahlan *nice to meet you*

asif *sorry*

ba*dak (*to man*); ba*dik (*to woman*) *after you*

Haraam *aleek! *that's very wrong, forbidden*

in sha' allah *God willing*

itfuhduhl (*to man*); itfuhduhlee (*to woman*) *come in; help yourself etc* (*literally – accept!*)

ɪwa *yes*

la' *no*

lowsamaHt *excuse me; please*

ma*alesh *never mind, it doesn't matter*

ma*a e-salemma *goodbye*

mabrook! *well done!, congratulations!*

mafeesh *there isn't any*

na*am *yes*

salamtak (*to man*); salamtik (*to woman*) *get well soon, I hope you feel better soon*

RESTAURANTS *see* NOTICES IN RESTAURANTS

REST ROOMS *see* TOILETS

ROAD SIGNS

مركز اسعاف ونجدة ambulance station

طريق متعرج bendy road

انتبه caution

نص المدينة city centre/center

خطر ممنوع الأنتظار dangerous: no parking

منحنيان عموديان الأول على اليمين double right hand bends ahead

ورشة garage

أولوية المرور في الميدان للقادم من

يمينك give priority to traffic from the right

الزم اليمين keep to the right

الدوران للخلف شمالا left turn only

طريق رئيسى main road

أقصى أرتفاع ٤ م maximum height 4m

أقصى عرض ٣م maximum width 3m

كوبرى ضيق narrow bridge

ممنوع مرور النقل no lorries/trucks

ممنوع السير من الجهتين no traffic at all

ممنوع الانتظار بين اليافطتين no waiting between the two signs

كوبرى ٦ اكتوبر October 6th Bridge

الانتظار موازى للرصيف park parallel to the pavement

موقف خصوصى private car park/parking lot

مزلقان سكك حديد railway/railroad crossing

مزلقان مقفول railway/railroad crossing with barriers

هدى السرعة reduce speed now

منحنى على اليمين right hand bend

منحنيات الأول على اليمين road bends first to the right

مطب road dips

مدرسة school

٦٠ كم /ساعة speed limit 60 km/h

منحدر خطر steep hill

قف STOP

امامك علامة قف stop at junction/intersection

قف . . التفتيش بعد ٣٠٠ متر traffic control ahead

السير في هذا الاتجاه traffic in this direction

مزلقان مفتوح unguarded railway/railroad crossing

ممنوع مرور السيارات التى يزيد وزنها على طنا unladen weight limit

ممنوع مرور السيارات التى تحمل اكثر من طنا ٥ , ٥ طن weight limit 5·5 tons

SCHEDULES *see* **TIMETABLES**

SHOP NAMES

مخبز *[makhbaz]* bakery

صالون تجميل *[salōn tagmeel]* beauty salon

مكتبة *[maktaba]* bookshop/bookstore and stationery

جزارة *[gizaarit ...]* butcher

أجزاخانة *[agzakhenna]* chemist, pharmacy

صيدلية [sIduhlaya] chemist, pharmacy

تحميض الأفلام الملونة [taHmeed el aflam el milowana] colo(u)r film processing

حلواني [Halawēnee] confectionery

ألبان [albān] dairy

مصبغة [muhsbuhgha] dry-cleaner

بقالة [bikaalit …] groceries

فطاطرى [fataatree] pastry shop/store

تصوير مستندات [tuhsweer mustanadet] photocopying

ستوديو [istudyo] photographer's studio

سوبر ماركت ['supermarket'] supermarket

STREETS

سكة [sikka] alley

كورنيش ['corniche'] corniche

زقاق [zoo'e'] cul-de-sac

عطفة [*atfa] lane

حارة [Haara] lane, alley

طريق [taree'] road

ميدان [midan] square

شارع [shāri*a] street

TAXIS

الأجرة [el ōgra] fare

أجرة [ōgra] for hire

حجز الليموزين [Hagz el 'limosine'] limousine service

تاكسى ['taxi'] taxi

موقف سيارات أجره [mow'af sIyaraat ōgra] taxi rank, taxi stand

TELEPHONES

سعر المكالمة [se*ar el mokalma] call charge

سعر الدقيقة بالقرش [se*ar e-duhkeeka bil kuhrsh] charge per minute in piastres

رقم الكود [rakuhm el 'code'] code number

دليل تليفونات تجارى [daleel telefonēt togaree] commercial telephone directory

مباشر للمحافظات [mobāshir lil moHafuhzaat] direct dial to other districts

دولى [dowlee] international

تليفون [telefōn] telephone

دليل تليفونات [daleel telefonēt] telephone directory

THEATRES, THEATERS

حجز تذاكر [Hagz tazēkir] advance bookings

كرسى بلكون [korsee balakōn] balcony seat

مسرح البالون [masraH el balloon] Balloon Theatre/Theater

(*Agooza*)

شباك تذاكر [shebek tazēkir] box office

مخرج [makhruhg] exit

السيرك القومى [e-sirk el kowmee] National Circus (*Agooza*)

المسرح القومى [el masraH el kowmee] National Theatre/Theater (*Ataba*)

مسرح العرائس [masraH el *ara'is] Puppet Theatre/Theater (*Ataba*)

يرفع الستار ٩ مساء [yorfa* e-sittar 9 misē' en] performance begins at 9 p.m.

أسعار الدخول [as*ar e-dikhool] price of admission

البرنامج [el birnāmig] program(me)

قاعة سيد درويش [ka*aIt sayyeed daroo-eesh] Sayyeed Daroo-eesh Concert Hall for Classical Arabic music

كرسى فوتيل [korsee footayl] seat in box

كرسى ممتاز [korsee momtaz] seat in circle

كرسى صالة [korsee saala] seat in stalls

ممنوع اصتحاب الكاميرات وأجهزة التسجيل [mamnoo-a* estiHaab el kamiraat wa ag-hezzit e-tazgeel] the use of cameras and

tape-recorders is prohibited

مسرح ... [masraH ...] ... theatre/theater

TIMETABLES, SCHEDULES

س	ق	hours	minutes
٧	٣٠	7	30

ميعاد الوصول [mee*ad el wisool] arrival time

درجات [daragaat] class

نوع القطار [no*a el kitaar] class of train

وقت القيام [wokt el keeyēm] departure time

ميعاد القيام [mee*ad el keeyēm] departure time

اكسبريس ['express'] express train

سياحى [seeyēHee] fast train with limited stops

مجرى [magaree] fast train with limited stops

درجة أولى [daraga oola] first class

ساعة [sa*a] hours

دقيقة [dikeeka; spoken: di'ee'a] minutes

لوكس [luks] pullman train

درجة ثانية [daraga tania] second class

جهة الوصول [gehat el wisool] terminates at ...

جدول المواعيد *[gadwil el mowa*id]* timetable, schedule

رقم القطار *[rakuhm el kitaar]* train number

TOILETS, REST ROOMS

للرجال *[lil rigāl]* gents, mens' rest rooms

للسيدات *[lil sIyeedat]* ladies, ladies' rest rooms

دورة المياه *[dowrit el meeyē]* toilet, rest room

دورات المياه *[dawaraat el meeyē]* toilets, rest rooms

TOURISM

حجز تذاكر ، طيران ـ بواخر *[Hagz tazēkir tIyaraan wa bawakhir]* advance booking for air and sea travel

تأجير سيارات وأتوبيسات فاخرة ومكيفة *[tageer sIyaraat wa ōtōbeeset fakheera wa mokIyefa]* car and bus rental service

رحلات يومية *[reHalat yomaya]* day trips

حجز فنادق *[Hagz fanādi']* hotel reservations

رحلات نيلية *[reHalat neelaya]* Nile Cruises

رحلات سياحية *[reHalat seeyaHaya]* package tours

YOUTH HOSTEL

بيت الشباب *[bayt e-shebab]* Youth Hostel

Reference Grammar

NOUNS

GENDER

Nouns in Arabic are either masculine or feminine. Feminine nouns are the easier to identify and can be divided into the following groups:

1. Most nouns ending in **-a**:

Haga	thing
shanta	bag

Nouns which form an exception to this rule (masculine nouns ending in **-a**) are indicated in the English-Arabic section of this book, for example:

dowa	medicine (*m*)

2. Some basically masculine nouns, often relating to professions, which have been extended to feminine use by the addition of the final **-a**:

doktor (*m*)	**doktora** (*f*)	doctor
garson (*m*)	**garsona** (*f*)	waiter/waitress

3. Nouns relating to something obviously feminine:

bint	girl
um	mother

4. Names of many countries and cities:

masr	Egypt
kaheera	Cairo

5. Names of many parts of the body:

ras	head
rigl	leg

These will be marked as feminine in the text.

6. There is a final (random) group of nouns which are unpredictably feminine. These will all be marked in the text. Some examples are:

shams	sun
feloos	money
da'n	beard

You can assume that all other nouns are masculine.

CONSTRUCT FORM

Some rules require the final **-a** of a feminine noun to be replaced by **-it**, for example, when two nouns are used together:

foota	towel
Hammem	bath
footit el Hammem	bath towel

PLURALS

There are three kinds of plurals in Arabic. They describe:

(a) two of anything
(b) three or more of anything
(c) collective groups of things

(a) *the dual plural*

This is formed by the addition of suffixes to the singular form.

For masculine nouns and irregular feminine nouns (not ending in **-a**) add **-ayn**, for example:

sing.		dual plural	
walad	boy	**waladayn**	two boys
eed	hand	**eedayn**	(two) hands

Feminine nouns ending in **-a** usually lose the final **-a** and then add **-tayn**, for example:

sing.		dual plural	
ezaza	bottle	**ezaztayn**	two bottles
kubbaya	cup	**kubbaytayn**	two cups
нaga	thing	**нagtayn**	two things

There are two variations to this rule. Some nouns do not lose the final **-a**, for example:

mara	one time, once
maratayn	two times, twice

And some nouns add **-ayn** to the construct form (see page 99):

shirka	company
shirkitayn	two companies

shanta	bag
shantitayn	two bags

(b) *the standard plural*

This is also formed by adding suffixes to the singular noun.

For masculine nouns add **-een**, for example:

fellaн	peasant farmer
fellaнeen	peasant farmers

For feminine nouns add **-at**, for example:

*agala	bicycle
*agalaat	bicycles

In the English-Arabic section of this book you will see the pronunciation of the feminine plural given variously as **-et**, **-at**, **-aat**, depending on the actual sound of a particular word, for example:

ōtōbeeset	buses
нagat	things
нasharaat	insects

(c) *the collective plural*

Strictly speaking this is a third form of certain nouns (together with the singular and plural). It is used to describe a whole class of items collectively and generally, for example:

mooz	bananas
bortoo'aan	oranges

The collective form is extremely useful for the tourist since it mainly concerns food. In particular, it is more widely used than either the singular or the standard plural for all fruits and vegetables. For this reason it is always shown under those headings in the Arabic-English section of this book as the form you are most likely to hear or read.

The singular can be formed from the collective by the addition of **-a**. For example:

collective	**batikh**	water melon *or* water melons
sing.	**batikha**	a water melon
plural	**talaat batikhaat**	three water melons

The word **bisella** (peas), on the other hand, is only likely to occur in the collective form.

Further examples of the collective form are:

bayd	eggs
samak	fish
sha*r	hair
shuhgar	trees

IRREGULAR PLURALS

A large number of Arabic nouns have irregular plurals. Here is a list of relevant irregular plurals that a traveller might commonly need to use.

sing.	plural		sing.	plural	
shanta	**shōnuht**	bag(s)	**ism**	**asēmee**	name(s)
bank	**binook**	bank(s)	**maktab**	**makētib**	office(s)
sireer	**sarayir**	bed(s)	**ōda**	**ewuhd**	room(s)
kitab	**kutub**	book(s)	**taabe*a**	**tawaabe*a**	stamp(s)
walad	**owlad**	boy(s)	**shari*a**	**shawēri*a**	street(s)
akh	**ekhwāt**	brother(s)	**taalib**	**tuhluhbba**	student(s)
gamal	**gimal**	camel(s)	**tazkara**	**tazēkir**	ticket(s)
sigara	**saggayar**	cigarette(s)	**medeena**	**modon**	town(s)
yum	**ıyēm**	day(s)	**atr**	**otora**	train(s)
saнib	**asнaab**	friend(s)	**isboo*a**	**asabee*a**	week(s)
bint	**banat**	girl(s)			
fondō'	**fanādi'**	hotel(s)			
bayt	**beeyoot**	house(s)			
muftaн	**mafateeн**	key(s)			
raagil	**rigālla**	man (man)			
di'ee'a	**da'ay'**	minute(s)			
shahr	**shihor**	month(s)			
gāmi*a	**gawēmi*a**	mosque(s)			
matнaf	**matēнif**	museum(s)			

ARTICLES

THE DEFINITE ARTICLE (THE)
The definite article is **el**. It precedes the noun and remains unchanged whether the noun is masculine, feminine, singular or plural.

However, in front of words beginning with the letters d, n, r, s, sh, t, z, and optionally g and k, the 'l' is assimilated and the initial consonant is lengthened during pronunciation. This is shown as **e-** so that the form of the original word remains obvious. For example:

el shams	⟶ **e-shams**	the sun
el raagil	⟶ **e-raagil**	the man

El may also be assimilated with several prepositions. For example:

bee/bi + el ⟶ **bil**	as in **bil atr** by train
fee/fi + el ⟶ **fil**	as in **fil baнr** in the sea **fil maya** per cent
lee/li + el ⟶ **lil**	as in **lil mattar** to the airport **lil balad** to town
*ala + el ⟶ ***alel**	as in ***alel bilasн** on the beach

THE INDEFINITE ARTICLE (A, AN)
There is no indefinite article in Arabic. The noun stands alone. For example:

ōtōbees	means 'bus' or 'a bus'
*arabaya	means 'car' or 'a car'
ōtōbeeset	means 'buses' or 'some buses'

ADJECTIVES

Adjectives follow the noun they describe and agree with the noun in gender and number, for example:

fondō' kwıyis	a good hotel
akla kwıyissa	a good meal

The feminine of adjectives is formed by adding **-a**, for example:

masculine	feminine
gameel **kebeer**	**gameela** **kebeera**

Occasionally the final consonant is doubled following a short vowel, for example:

masculine	feminine
kwıyis	**kwıyissa**

Adjectives ending in **-ee** are invariable and do not change their form whether they are used with masculine or feminine nouns, for example:

gurnaan ingileezee	an English newspaper
***arabaya ingileezee**	an English car

Note that if you use 'very' with an adjective then the Arabic word for 'very' always follows the adjective it qualifies, for example:

akla kwɪyissa awee	a very good meal

If the definite article is used then it must occur twice – once in front of the noun and once in front of any adjective that goes with the noun, for example:

el maнatta e-ra'eesaya	the main station
e-raagil el *agooz	the old man
el 'consul' el breetaanee	the British Consul

ADJECTIVES AND PLURAL NOUNS

(a) If a plural noun, masculine or feminine, refers to humans then a plural adjective must be used. This can be formed by adding **-een** to the singular adjective, for example:

sing.	plural
kwɪyis	**kwɪyiseen**
nas kwɪyiseen	nice people

(b) If a plural noun refers to inanimate objects then the adjective takes the feminine singular form (regardless of the gender of the original noun), for example:

feminine	**mabēnee kebeera**	large buildings
masculine	**fanadi' kebeera**	large hotels

(c) A dual plural noun should always be followed by a plural adjective, for example:

mabnayayn kubaar	two large buildings

IRREGULAR PLURAL ADJECTIVES

Many plural adjectives are irregular. Here is a list of the commoner ones:

sing.	plural	
kebeer	**kubaar**	large
sooghɪyar	**sooghaar**	small
shedeed	**shudād**	strong
rakhees	**rokhaas**	cheap
adeem	**odam**	old (*not used for people*)
gameel	**goomal**	beautiful
nedeef	**nudaf**	clean

COMPARATIVES AND SUPERLATIVES (BIGGER, BIGGEST etc)

The comparative and superlative forms of the adjective are the same. They also remain the same for either sex or number.

Common comparative and superlative adjectives are:

ADJ	COMP/SUPER	
kebeer	akbar	bigger/biggest
sooghɪyar	uhsgar	smaller/smallest
ghêlee	eghla	more/most expensive
rekhees	arkhuhs	cheaper/cheapest
gameel	agmal	more/most beautiful
Helw	aHla	nicer/nicest; prettier/prettiest
kwɪyis	aHsen	better/best
keteer	aktar	more/most

For example:

| **fondō' akbar** | a bigger hotel |
| **el fondō' el akbar** | the bigger/biggest hotel |

To compare two things in Arabic you simply use the comparative form of the adjective + **min**, for example:

akbar min
bigger than

el kaheera akbar min el ĺu'sor
Cairo is bigger than Luxor

To express a superlative meaning you simply reverse the word order, i.e.:

comparative adjective + noun (without the article)

For example:

| **akbar haram** | the biggest pyramid |
| **aHsen fondō'** | the best hotel |

DEMONSTRATIVE ADJECTIVES (THIS, THAT, THESE, THOSE)

The demonstrative adjectives are:

da	*(masculine singular)*	this/that
dee	*(feminine singular)*	this/that
dol	*(masc. and fem. plurals)*	these/those

They follow **el** + noun, for example:

e-raagil da	this/that man
el bint dee	this/that girl
e-nas dol	these/those people

POSSESSIVE ADJECTIVES (MY, YOUR etc)

There are no possessive adjectives as in English. Instead, Arabic adds suffixes to the noun. They are added directly to a masculine noun or to the construct form of a feminine noun, where the **-a** has been replaced by **-it** (see page 99).

The suffix varies according to the number or gender of the possessor, for example:

noun + **ee**	my
noun + **ak**	your (*masc. sing.*)
noun + **ik**	your (*fem. sing.*)
noun + **oo**	his
noun + **ha**	her
noun + **na**	our
noun + **koo**	your (*plural*)
noun + **hum**	their

shantitee	my bag
umak	your mother (*said to a man*)
umik	your mother (*said to a woman*)
baytna	our house
***ınwãnhum**	their address

Possession can also be shown by using **bita*** (of). This must also be made to agree in gender and number with the possessor, as above. It also varies with the gender of the thing which is possessed.

object masculine	object feminine	
bita*ee	**bita*tee**	my
bita*ak	**bita*tak**	your (*owner masculine*)
bita*ik	**bita*tik**	your (*owner feminine*)
bita*oo	**bita*too**	his
bita*ha	**bita*t-ha**	her
bita*ana	**bita*tna**	our
bita*akoo	**bita*tkoo**	your
bita*ahum	**bita*t-hum**	their

The word **bita*** follows the noun and requires the definite article **el** in front of the noun, for example:

e-shanta bita*tee	my bag
el bayt bita*ee	my house

Note that **bita*** should not be used for people. For example, to say 'my brother' you must use the suffix form of the possessive.

But **bita*** should always be used with any word that has been borrowed from another language. These words often appear in the text of this book in inverted commas, for example:

el 'camera' bita*tee	my camera

Pronouns

PRONOUNS

PERSONAL PRONOUNS

Personal pronouns which replace the subject of a sentence (I, you etc) exist in Arabic as independent words. Personal pronouns functioning as a direct object (me, you etc) or as an indirect object (to me, to you etc) take the form of suffixes to the verb. Here is a list of personal pronouns.

SUBJECT		DIRECT OBJECT		INDIRECT OBJECT	
ana	I	verb + **nee**	me	verb + **nee**	to me
inta	you (*m*)	verb + **ak**	you (*m*)	verb + **lak**	to you (*m*)
intee	you (*f*)	verb + **ik**	you (*f*)	verb + **lik**	to you (*f*)
hoowa	he/it	verb + **oo**	him/it	verb + **loo**	to him/it
haya	she/it	verb + **ha**	her/it	verb + **lha**	to her/it
eнna	we	verb + **na**	us	verb + **lna**	to us
intoo	you (*pl*)	verb + **koo**	you (*pl*)	verb + **lkoo**	to you (*pl*)
humma	they	verb + **hum**	them	verb + **lahum**	to them

sibtaha hena
I left it here   (*object feminine*)

sibtoo hena
I left it here   (*object masculine*)

shuftuhum e-naharda e-subн
I saw them this morning

Note that in Arabic subject pronouns may be omitted when the conjugation of the verb makes them superfluous. **Ana** (I) is the most likely to be omitted, as in the examples above.

When a sentence contains both direct and indirect objects the order will be the same as in English, i.e. verb + direct object + indirect object, for example:

eddeehanee!   give it to me!

REFLEXIVE PRONOUNS (MYSELF, YOURSELF etc)
Reflexive pronouns are:

nafsee	myself
nafsak	yourself (*masculine sing.*)
nafsik	yourself (*feminine sing.*)
nafsoo	himself
nafsaha	herself
nafsinna	ourselves
nafsukoo	yourselves
nafsoohu	themselves

a*miloo binafsak   do it yourself

USE OF PRONOUNS WITH PREPOSITIONS

Pronouns frequently occur suffixed to prepositions. They then follow a set pattern depending on whether the preposition ends with a vowel or a consonant, for example:

*alashēn (for)   **ma*a** (with)

*alashen-ee	for me	**ma*a-ya**	with me
-ak	for you (*masc.*)	**-k**	with you (*masc.*)
-ik	for you (*fem.*)	**-ki**	with you (*fem.*)
-oo	for him	**-h**	with him
-ha	for her	**-ha**	with her
-na	for us	**-na**	with us
-koo	for you (*pl.*)	**-koo**	with you (*pl.*)
-hum	for them	**-hum**	with them

The same endings can be used with these words:

min (from)   **zay** (like)   ***ala** (on/against)

da minee   that's from me
haya zayik   she's like you
da *alashenna?   is that for us?

You will often find them used in very colloquial phrases, for example:

ma*ak kabreet?   have you got any matches?
                                  (literally: matches with you?)

In fact, ***and** (at) + suffixed pronoun is even used in place of the verb 'to have' — which does not exist in Arabic. See page 114.

DEMONSTRATIVE PRONOUNS (THIS, THAT, THESE, THOSE)

The demonstrative pronouns are the same as the demonstrative adjectives:

da	(*masculine singular*)	this/that
dee	(*feminine singular*)	this/that
dol	(*masc. and fem. plural*)	these/those

They must agree in number and gender with the noun they are replacing and precede it in a sentence (as in English), for example:

da fondō' kwɪyis   that's a good hotel
dee *arabeetee   that's my car
mumkin dee/da?   can I have that one?
dee/da aʜsen   that's better

Where gender is unspecified, as in the last examples above, then either **dee** or **da** may be used although the feminine **dee** is probably the more likely.

POSSESSIVE PRONOUNS (MINE, YOURS etc)

These are the same as the suffixed forms of **bita*** which can be used in place of possessive adjectives.

object masculine   *object feminine*

bita*ee	**bita*tee**	mine
bita*ak	**bita*tak**	yours (*owner masculine*)
bita*ik	**bita*tik**	yours (*owner feminine*)
bita*oo	**bita*too**	his
bita*ha	**bita*t-ha**	hers
bita*ana	**bita*tna**	ours
bita*akoo	**bita*tkoo**	yours
bita*ahum	**bita*t-hum**	theirs

e-shanta bita*tee	the bag's mine
da bita*ee!	that's mine!

Note that the first example could also mean 'my bag'.

OF

Phrases such as 'the address of the hotel' are expressed as follows:

noun (possessed) + el + noun (possessor)

For example:

*ɪnwăn el fondō'	the address of the hotel
wa't e-reʜla	the time of the flight
ism e-shari*a	the name of the street

Feminine nouns (as the possessed) appear in the construct form (**-a** becomes **-it**, see page 99), for example:

shantit el bint	the girl's handbag
odit bintee	my daughter's room

To make the phrase indefinite simply omit the article, for example:

ʜettit *ɪ-esh	a piece of bread
kubbayit shay	a cup of tea

The rule is the same with proper nouns, for example:

bayt aʜmad	Ahmed's house
medeenit el iskindraya	the city of Alexandria

VERBS

THE INFINITIVE (TO LIKE, TO EAT etc)
There is no infinitive in Arabic. Instead, the verb is recognized by the form taken by the 3rd person singular in the perfect tense. This form is shown in column 1 of the table of Arabic verbs below, for example:

Habb he liked   **kal** he ate

This is how Arabic verbs are represented in dictionaries and the English-Arabic section of this book follows this convention.

When translating English sentences containing an infinitive, both verbs must agree with the subject. For example:

*a-ızeen nerooн lee ...   we want to go to ...
                                       (literally: we want we go to ...)

TABLE OF COMMON ARABIC VERBS
This table shows the two Arabic tenses in the first person singular, or 'I' form, which is the form you are most likely to need in conversation.

1 Infinitive equivalent ('he' form, perfect tense)	2 'I' form IMPERFECT	3 'I' form PERFECT	
sa'al	as'al	sa'alt	to ask
	kunt		to be †
aydir	a'dar	aydirt	to be able to
beda'a	abda	beda'at	to begin
gab	ageeb	gibt	to bring
ishtera	ashteree	ishtereet	to buy
ga	agee	gayt	to come †
shirib	ashrab	shribt	to drink
kal	akul	kalt	to eat
edda	addee	idayt	to give
raн	arooн	roнt	to go †
	*andee		to have †
*arif	a*aruhf	*arift	to know
нabb	aнebb	нabbayt	to like/love
buhss	aboss	buhseet	to look
*amal	a*mil	*amalt	to make/do
нuhtt	aнott	нattayt	to put
al	a'ool	olt	to say/tell
shuf	ashoof	shuft	to see
nam	anām	nimt	to sleep
kallim	atkallim	kallimt	to speak
khad	akhud	khat	to take
fakar	afakuhr	fakart	to think
fehim	afham	fehimt	to understand †
mishee	imshee	misheet	to walk, go away
	*a-ıyiz		to want †
ishtaghel	ashtaghel	ishtaghelt	to work

† see page 113-115

TENSES

Strictly speaking there are only two tenses of the verb: the imperfect (used for incomplete action in the *present* or the *future*) and the perfect (for completed action in the *past*).

However, colloquial Egyptian Arabic can make a distinction between present and future usage of the imperfect tense by the addition of extra prefixes (see below).

IMPERFECT TENSE

The imperfect tense is formed by adding prefixes and suffixes to a verb stem. You can work out the stem by removing the initial **a** from the 'I' form in column 2 of the verb table above. For example:

aнebb gives the stem **нebb**

The verb is conjugated by adding the following prefixes and suffixes to the stem:

a____	**aнebb**	I like
ti____	**tiнebb**	you like (*masc. sing.*)
ti____ee	**tiнebbee**	you like (*fem. sing.*)
yi____	**yiнebb**	he likes
ti____	**tiнebb**	she likes
ni____	**niнebb**	we like
ti____oo	**tiнebboo**	you like (*plural*)
yi____oo	**yiнebboo**	they like

In practice and in this book, you may find the first vowel is pronounced or transliterated as **e** or **i** in different verbs, depending on the actual sound of the word. However, the grammatical process is constant.

PRESENT USAGE OF THE IMPERFECT TENSE

The imperfect conjugation can be used for the present tense. In colloquial Egyptian Arabic the prefix **bi-** is added to the imperfect tense to make it clear that the action of a verb is in the present, for example:

baнebb †	I like
bitнebb	you like (*masc. sing.*)
bitнebbee	you like (*fem. sing.*)
biнebb	he likes
bitнebb	she likes
binнebb	we like
bitнebboo	you like (*plural*)
biнebboo	they like

† The **i** is not heard here in spoken Arabic.

Note the elision of the second vowel in typical native speech where **bitiнebb** becomes **bitнebb**. If you neglect to do this you will still be understood.

FUTURE USAGE OF THE IMPERFECT TENSE (I WILL, YOU WILL etc)

The imperfect tense can also be modified to show that the action will occur in the future by adding the prefix **нa-** to the stem, for example:

нанebb	I will like
наthebb	you will like (*masc. sing.*)
натнebbee	you will like (*fem. sing.*)
нінebb †	he will like
натнebb	she will like
наннebb	we will like
натнebboo	you will like (*plural*)
нінebboo †	they will like

† The sound changes in spoken Arabic.

PERFECT TENSE (I ATE, I HAVE EATEN etc)
The perfect tense is used for completed action in the past. It is used for both the simple past and the perfect tense in English. For example:

ana shuftoo   translates as   I saw him/I have seen him

The perfect tense is formed by adding suffixes to a verb stem (except in the case of the third person masculine singular 'he'). To find the stem, remove the final **t** from the verb form shown in column 3 of the verb table on page 109. For example **kallim** is the perfect stem for the verb 'to speak'.

For the third person masculine or 'he' form, use the word in column 1 of the verb table (page 109) (or the first translation in the English-Arabic section of this book).

Most verbs are conjugated as follows:

-t	kallimt	I spoke/have spoken
-t	kallimt	you spoke/have spoken (*masc. sing.*)
-tee	kallimtee	you spoke/have spoken (*fem. sing.*)
-	kallim	he spoke/has spoken
-it	kallimit	she spoke/has spoken
-na	kallimna	we spoke/have spoken
-too	kallimtoo	you spoke/have spoken (*plural*)
-oo	kallimoo	they spoke/have spoken

Exceptions

(a) to give, to like, to put. For these verbs, remove **-ayt** from the word in column 3 (page 109) to find the stem and then add the following suffixes:

-ayt	idayt	I gave/have given
-ayt	idayt	you gave/have given (*masc. sing.*)
-aytee	idaytee	you gave/have given (*fem. sing.*)
-	edda	he gave/has given
-it	idit	she gave/has given
-ayna	idayna	we have/have given
-aytoo	idaytoo	you gave/have given (*plural*)
-oo	idoo	they gave/have given

(b) to buy, to look, to go away. For these verbs, remove **-eet** from the word in column 3 (page 109) to find the stem and then add the following suffixes:

-eet	ishtereet	I bought/have bought
-eet	ishtereet	you bought/have bought (*masc. sing.*)
-eetee	ishtereetee	you bought/have bought (*fem. sing.*)
-	ishtera	he bought/has bought
-it	ishterit	she bought/has bought
-eena	ishtereena	we bought/have bought
-eetoo	ishtereetoo	you bought/have bought (*plural*)
-oo	ishteroo	they bought/have bought

MAKING THE VERB NEGATIVE

The negative is formed by joining **ma** to the front of the verb and adding **sh** to the end, for example:

mabadakhansh	I don't smoke
ma*andeesh	I haven't got

This can sometimes result in a very long word. If you find this difficult to form at first, another way of making a verb negative is by using the word **mush** in front of the verb, for example:

mush *aruhf	I don't know
or **ma*arafsh**	

There are a few 'verbs' which only use the **mush** version of the negative. These include 'to want' and the alternative forms taken in the present by 'to go', 'to come' and 'to understand'.

mush *a-ɪyiz ʜaga	I don't want anything
mush fehim	I don't understand

THE IMPERATIVE (GIVING COMMANDS)

To form an imperative omit the initial **t** from the second person singular or plural of the verb in the imperfect tense, for example:

eshrab!	drink up!
eddeehanee	give it to me

Some other useful imperatives are:

estanna hena	stay here
imshee!	go away!
o'af!	stop!
ta*ala hena	come here

To form the negative imperative (don't ...) take the second person singular or plural of the verb in the imperfect tense and add **ma-** at the front and **-sh** at the end, for example:

mato'afsh!	don't stop!
matestannash	don't wait

QUESTIONS

In Arabic the word order of a question is identical to that of the corresponding statement, for example:

inta *a-ɪyiz нaga	you want something
inta *a-ɪyiz нaga?	do you want something?

The difference is marked by using the same intonation at the end as you would in an English question.

INTERROGATIVE WORDS

Words such as:

fayn?	where?	**lay?**	why?
emta?	when?	**izzay?**	how?

are usually placed at the end of a question. They do, however, also occur at the beginning, sometimes for emphasis, for example:

el maнatta fayn?	where is the station?
or **fayn el maнatta?**	

IRREGULAR VERBS

There are very few irregular verbs in Arabic. However there are several words used in a verbal sense which are not 'grammatically' verbs at all. These exceptional cases, which all translate into very common verbs in English, are given below.

TO BE

There is no equivalent to the present tense of the verb 'to be' (am/is/are) in Arabic.

Simple sentences in which forms of the verb 'to be' occur do not require a verb in Arabic. Some examples follow:

tazkartak fayn?	where is your ticket?
e-gow gameel e-naharda	the weather's lovely today
ana mabsoot awee	I'm very happy
el mat*am da kwɪyis?	is this restaurant any good?

In the past tense the verb 'to be' is conjugated as follows:

ana kunt	I was
inta kunt	you were (*masc. sing.*)
intee kuntee	you were (*fem. sing.*)
hoowa kan	he was
haya kanit	she was
eнna kunna	we were
intoo kuntoo	you were (*plural*)
humma kanoo	they were

For example:

kunt fayn?	where were you?

Negatives are formed in the standard way:

ana makuntish	I wasn't
hoowa makansh	he wasn't
etc	

Note also:

fee	there is/are
mafeesh	there isn't/aren't
kan fee	there was/were
makansh fee	there wasn't/weren't

TO HAVE

The preposition ***and** is used with the appropriate suffixes:

*andee	I have
*andak	you have (*masc. sing.*)
*andik	you have (*fem. sing.*)
*andoo	he has
*andaha	she has
*andenna	we have
*andukoo	you have (*plural*)
*anduhum	they have

The future tense is formed by placing the word ʜɪkoon in front of the word for 'have', for example:

ʜɪ**koon *andak**   you will have

The past tense is formed by placing **kan** in front, for example:

kan *andak   you had

TO WANT

(a) present tense

In the present tense all singular forms are represented by:

*a-ɪyiz   (*if subject masculine*)
*a-ɪza   (*if subject feminine*)

All plural forms are represented by:

   *a-ɪzeen

Negatives are formed by placing **mush** in front, for example:

   mush *a-ɪyiz   I don't want (to), he doesn't want (to)

(b) the past tense

kunt *a-ɪyiz	I wanted (*masc.*)
kunt *a-ɪza	I wanted (*fem.*)
kunt *a-ɪyiz	you wanted (*masc.*)
kuntee *a-ɪza	you wanted (*fem.*)
kan *a-ɪyiz	he wanted
kanit *a-ɪza	she wanted
kunna *a-ɪzeen	we wanted
kuntoo *a-ɪzeen	you wanted (*plural*)
kanoo *a-ɪzeen	they wanted

The negative is formed thus:

> **makuntish *a-ıyiz**   I didn't want (to)
> **makansh *a-ıyiz**   he didn't want (to)

TO COME, TO GO, TO UNDERSTAND

As alternatives to the present tense of these verbs the following participles are frequently used. Although they are not actually 'verbs', they have verbal meaning:

	come	go	understand
all masc. sing. forms	**gay**	**rıaн**	**fēhim**
all fem. sing. forms	**gaya**	**rıнa**	**fēhma**
all plural forms	**gayeen**	**rıнeen**	**fēhmeen**

For example:

> **ana rıaн**   I'm going
> **inta gay?**   are you coming?

To make these negative place **mush** in front of the participle, for example:

> **ana mush rıaн**   I'm not going

TELLING THE TIME

what time is it?	e-sa*a kam?
it is ...	'it is' does not occur on its own in Egyptian Arabic
(it is) one o'clock	e-sa*a waнda
(it is) seven o'clock	e-sa*a sab*a
one a.m.	e-sa*a waнda e-subн
seven a.m.	e-sa*a sab*a e-subн
one p.m.	e-sa*a waнda ba*d e-dohr (ba*d e-dohr means 'in the afternoon')
seven p.m.	e-sa*a sab*a bil layl (bil layl means 'in the evening')
midday	e-dohr
midnight	nus el layl
five past eight	e-sa*a tamania wi khamsa
five to eight	e-sa*a tamania illa khamsa
half past ten	e-sa*a *ashara wi nus
quarter past eleven	e-sa*a нidaashar wi rub*a
quarter to eleven	e-sa*a нidaashar illa rub*a
five past	wi khamsa
ten past	wi *ashara
quarter past	wi rub*a
twenty past	wi tilt
twenty five past	wi nus illa khamsa
half past	wi nus
twenty five to	wi nus wi khamsa
twenty to	illa tilt
quarter to	illa rub*a
ten to	illa *ashara
five to	illa khamsa

CONVERSION TABLES

1. LENGTH

centimetres, centimeters
1 cm = 0.39 inches

metres, meters
1 m = 100 cm = 1000 mm
1 m = 39.37 inches = 1.09 yards

kilometres, kilometers
1 km = 1000 m
1 km = 0.62 miles = 5/8 mile

km	1	2	3	4	5	10	20	30	40	50	100
miles	0.6	1.2	1.9	2.5	3.1	6.2	12.4	18.6	24.9	31.1	62.1

inches
1 inch = 2.54 cm

feet
1 foot = 30.48 cm

yards
1 yard = 0.91 m

miles
1 mile = 1.61 km = 8/5 km

miles	1	2	3	4	5	10	20	30	40	50	100
km	1.6	3.2	4.8	6.4	8.0	16.1	32.2	48.3	64.4	80.5	161

2. WEIGHT

gram(me)s
1 g = 0.035 oz

g	100	250	500
oz	3.5	8.75	17.5 = 1.1 lb

kilos

1 kg = 1000 g
1 kg = 2.20 lb = 11/5 lb

kg	0.5	1	1.5	2	3	4	5	6	7	8	9	10
lb	1.1	2.2	3.3	4.4	6.6	8.8	11.0	13.2	15.4	17.6	19.8	22

kg	20	30	40	50	60	70	80	90	100
lb	44	66	88	110	132	154	176	198	220

tons

1 UK ton = 1018 kg
1 US ton = 909 kg

tonnes

1 tonne = 1000 kg
1 tonne = 0.98 UK tons = 1.10 US tons

ounces

1 oz = 28.35 g

pounds

1 pound = 0.45 kg = 5/11 kg

lb	1	1.5	2	3	4	5	6	7	8	9	10	20
kg	0.5	0.7	0.9	1.4	1.8	2.3	2.7	3.2	3.6	4.1	4.5	9.1

stones

1 stone = 6.35 kg

stones	1	2	3	7	8	9	10	11	12	13	14	15
kg	6.3	12.7	19	44	51	57	63	70	76	83	89	95

hundredweights

1 UK hundredweight = 50.8 kg
1 US hundredweight = 45.36 kg

3. CAPACITY

litres, liters

1 l = 1.76 UK pints = 2.13 US pints
½ l = 500 cl
¼ l = 250 cl

pints
1 UK pint = 0.57 l
1 US pint = 0.47 l

quarts
1 UK quart = 1.14 l
1 US quart = 0.95 l

gallons
1 UK gallon = 4.55 l
1 US gallon = 3.79 l

4. TEMPERATURE

centigrade/Celsius
C = (F − 32) × 5/9

C	−5	0	5	10	15	18	20	25	30	37	38
F	23	32	41	50	59	64	68	77	86	98.4	100.4

Fahrenheit
F = (C × 9/5) + 32

F	23	32	40	50	60	65	70	80	85	98.4	101
C	−5	0	4	10	16	20	21	27	30	37	38.3

NUMBERS

•	0	sifr	٥١	51	waaHid wi khamseen
١	1	waaHid; *(for feminine nouns)* waHda	٦•	60	sitteen
			٧•	70	sab*een
			٨•	80	tamaneen
٢	2	itneen	٩•	90	tis*een
٣	3	talaata	١••	100	maya
٤	4	arba*a	١•١	101	maya waaHid
٥	5	khamsa	١•٢	102	maya witneen
٦	6	sitta	١•٣	103	maya wi talaata
٧	7	sab*a	١•٤	104	maya warba*a
٨	8	tamania	١•٥	105	maya wi khamsa
٩	9	tis*a	٢••	200	mitayn
١•	10	*ashara	٣••	300	tultoomaya
١١	11	Hidaashar	٤••	400	rub*amaya
١٢	12	itnaashar	٥••	500	khumsoomaya
١٣	13	talattaashar	٦••	600	sittoomaya
١٤	14	arba*taashar	٧••	700	sub*amaya
١٥	15	khamastaashar	٨••	800	tomnoomaya
١٦	16	sittaashar	٩••	900	tis*a-oomaya
١٧	17	saba*taashar	١•••	1000	alf
١٨	18	tamantaashar	٢•••	2000	alfayn
١٩	19	tisa*taashar	٣•••	3000	talaat talef
٢•	20	*ashreen	٤•••	4000	arba* talef
٢١	21	waaHid wa *ashreen	١٩٨٨	1988	alf tis*a-oomaya tamania wi tamaneen
٢٢	22	itneen wa *ashreen			
٢٣	23	talaata wa *ashreen			

		masculine	feminine
٢٤	24	arba*a wa *ashreen		
٢٥	25	khamsa wa *ashreen		
٢٦	26	sitta wa *ashreen	1st	*el owel*	*el oola*
٢٧	27	sab*a wa *ashreen	2nd	*e-tanee*	*e-tania*
٢٨	28	tamania wa *ashreen	3rd	*e-taalet*	*e-talta*
٢٩	29	tis*a wa *ashreen	4th	*e-rabia**	*e-raba**
٣•	30	talateen	5th	*el khamis*	*el khamsa*
٣١	31	waaHid wi talateen	6th	*es-saddis*	*es-sadsa*
٣٢	32	itneen wi talateen	7th	*es-sabia**	*es-saba*a*
٤•	40	arba*een	8th	*e-tamen*	*e-tamna*
٤١	41	waaHid wa arba*een	9th	*e-tassia**	*e-tassa*a*
٥•	50	khamseen	10th	*el *asher*	*el *ashara*